COPPER COBRA

A Pedro the Water Dog Saves the Planet Primer

AVIS KALFSBEEK

Download the FREE *Sexy Salmon with Camas Guide* for resources on fishing and protecting Bristol Bay: www.AvisKalfsbeek.com/SexySalmon

Acknowledgments:
Patreon Patrons
Benjamin Katz Creative
Todd Boston Music

ISBN 978-1-7355613-9-4 (First Edition Hardback)
ISBN 978-1-978965-00-4 (First Edition Paperback)
ISBN 978-1-953965-01-1 (Ebook)

www.AvisKalfsbeek.com

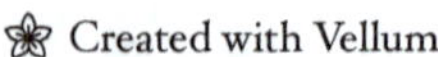

For the Alaska Native people, including the Yup'ik, Dena'ina, and Alutiiq, and other individuals who work tirelessly to protect Bristol Bay and the beauty of its natural environment and all of its inhabitants

"Only a major shift in moral reasoning, with greater commitment given to the rest of life, can meet this greatest challenge of the century."
–E.O. Wilson

Camas's **Raise it red!** *scenes with reference to poisonous runoff from mines is taken from real-life EPA reports.*

CHAPTER 1
WALLEYE POLLOCK {THERAGRA CHALCOGRAMMA}

The vivid green of the treeless Alaskan tundra seems to go on forever with streams winding artfully throughout the vast landscape of dwarf shrubs, herbs, grasses, mosses, lichens, and scattered wildflowers under an endless blue sky. On a summer morning in a modern time, when many say the earth will eventually not sustain its humans, a bright red salmon jumps energetically out of a sparkling, fast-moving stream. The water rushes over round rocks until the stream falls quickly down a rushing waterfall as sockeye salmon race up in bouncy leaps by the thousands. Buoyed by the energetic music of the electricity in their DNA calling them home, they race up and up the falls as an immense grizzly bear waits near the top, her two cubs playing on the nearby bank. A shimmering, red sockeye salmon leaps into the falls. It disappears for a moment then reappears as the bear lunges to catch it in her white fangs.

A forked, spear-like tool, held by Tana, a sturdy woman in her thirties with brunette hair pulled back in a ponytail under a knit cap, comes down on the head of a live salmon on a commercial fishing boat deck. She is surrounded by frenetic activity as hundreds of fish are reeled onto the boat stuck in a large net. Captain Jake Selkirk, a tall, good-looking, mountain-sized man in his late 50s, with a big, handsome smile wearing a knit beanie over his receding hairline, shouts commands. Moore, a slender young man with short dark hair and boyish handsomeness, and Jake's first mate, Iditarod, a rugged man in his fifties with a weathered face, beard, and mustache, maneuver the reel machinery to pull a large net of fish onto the boat. The crew wears bright orange fisherman overalls and gloves. Spit, Moore's best friend, with surfer-like, shoulder-length blonde hair, throws fish rapidly into an iced chamber. They continue the strenuous work at full speed despite exhaustion. From a bird's-eye view, Jake's boat sits among hundreds of commercial fishing boats in Bristle Bay, at the mouth of the Kojak River.

Fishing boats swarm a very productive, crowded area of the bay. Captains call commands to their crews, and boats dance with each other to optimize their catch. Jake's net extends out near the fishing boundary delineated by the Department of Fish and Game. The fish are bountiful, and Rod, Moore, Spit, and Tana move around the boat in preparation to receive Jake's call to pull in the net.

"Tana, come clean the goddamn windows!"

"Yes, sir!" Tana shouts as she races up the stairs to squeegee the windows with an anti-fog solution.

"The net's lit up with reds, but you're right on the boundary, captain!" Rod shouts.

"Shit!" Jake puts the boat in reverse, careful not to back up over the net. "I could stay on this line forever the way it's hitting, but I've had enough of those $5,000 Fish and Game fines over the years," he says to Tana as she cleans.

A large state-of-the-art fishing boat comes screaming dangerously along the border, headed straight towards Jake's vessel.

"What's that crazy bastard doing now?" Jake says, grimacing.

The crew turns to look.

Torden, a tall, handsome man with short blonde hair in his mid-thirties, stands at the wheel and accelerates just behind Jake's boat. It appears he is going to crash into it, but he makes a quick turn and flies quickly out over the boundary line and back inside.

Torden looks back to his crew and shouts, "Let her go!"

Torden's crew moves at lightning speed to release the net as the boat circles back and lands just in front of Jake, his net intercepting Jake's harvest.

"That son of a bitch!"

Jake's face is red with anger.

"Wow! How'd he do that?" Spit asks with eyes wide.

"He's retrofitted his boat to achieve more lift and speed. You know how you see birds flying just above the water?" Tana asks.

"Yeah. Ground effect?" Moore asks.

Rod raises his eyebrows; impressed Moore knows the term.

"Exactly," Tana nods.

"People thought he was crazy. Still do. He paid someone an enormous amount, almost the same cost as his expensive boat, to make a foil skirt to reduce drag and raise the boat out of the water without knowing if it would work," Rod adds.

"It works," Moore says, impressed.

Jake raises the fish club blade over his head in the stance of warrior Poseidon pointing it towards Torden. Torden laughs, dismissing him. His crew continues fishing the line.

"Jake seems super pissed," Spit says.

"He hates getting corked, but the truth is, Jake was that guy twenty-five years ago, fishing fast, greedy and intense. Top fisherman by whatever means necessary. He's mellowed." Rod says.

Moore looks up at the captain holding the club. "That's mellow?"

CHAPTER 2
SABLEFISH {ANOPLOPOMA FIMBRIA}

Thomas Foolerin, a young black man in his twenties, with short bleached blond hair, stands reading a poem on a small stage in a dark, cozy dive bar in Washington DC. He wears a beret, an untucked, vintage, long-sleeved collared shirt over a white T-shirt, Levi jeans with a 4-inch cuff, and laced boots. The room has a few people at the bar and a handful of people sitting at tables. A few are listening; most are in conversations.

Thomas reads Rachel Carson in a beat poet rhythm with a snap of his fingers to accent.

"Within two days, dead and dying fish, including many young salmon...

(*snap snap*)

Were found dead along the banks of the stream. Brook trout also appeared... among the dead fish.

(*snap*)

And along the roads and in the woods, birds were dying. All of the life of the stream...

(*snap snap*)

was stilled. Amid such a picture of destruction, the young salmon

(*snap*)

Could hardly have been expected… to escape

(*snap*)

And they did not.

Thomas, wearing a dark, olive green, houndstooth suit with a neon green tie, stands outside the Senate Chamber of the United States Capitol, talking to a senator. He points to an open report in his hand.

Dew Plicitus, an older man in his fifties, with a stark, a white-tipped, pointed goatee with wavy, slicked-back salt and pepper hair wearing a black suit with a bright red tie, walks past. He notices Thomas and throws a disdainful scowl in his direction.

Prewitt Mountain, a small, balding man in his sixties wearing small-frame glasses and a suit, walks into a sterile office with stacks and stacks of reports on tables lining the wall. A young woman, Reina McCaring, in her thirties, with short, wavy blond hair and black-framed glasses, sits hunched over some papers in the center of a table, the stacks tall above her on either side and an old black-and-white photograph of a fleet of sailing fishing boats on Bristle Bay hanging above her on the wall.

"What are you reading?" Prewitt asks.

"The scientific research studies on Copper Cobra. I'm 34.678 percent through."

"Well, you can bag that project."

"Oh, thank goodness! The permit's revoked!"

"Hell no. We got the word from Whiskey Hotel to fast track it."

"I'll try to read faster, sir. The fact that it's even in permitting is a sacrilege."

"Reina, the only thing sacred is my job as director of the EPA."

"What does the Army Corps of Engineers say?"

"They just hired Beatrice Laurels in diapers as the Environmental Chief to approve the 404 permit."

"Young doesn't mean corrupt."

"Let's just say... she's malleable."

"We've got boatloads of data to stop the mine. I'll go faster."

"Bea's been told to fast track the approval, so that means *we're* fast-tracking the approval. You can stop your egg head reading."

Prewitt walks out. Reina has a beautiful photograph of sockeye swimming in aqua blue water lying on her desk. She slumps down, her head resting wearily on top of the photo.

CHAPTER 3
PACIFIC HERRING
{THALEICHTHY PACIFUS}

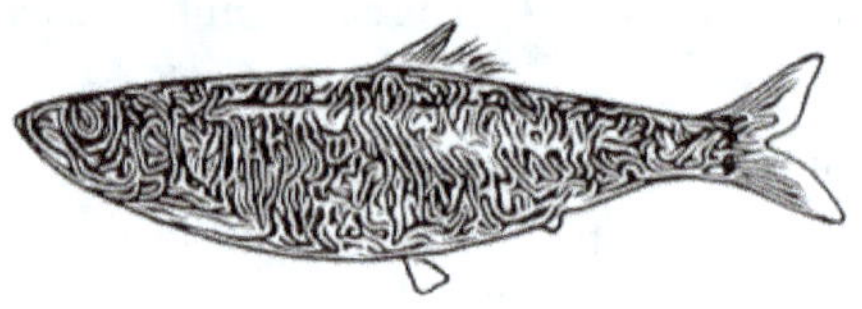

A river mouth, fish-kissing mouth, and *you-kiss-your-mother-with-that-mouth montage* reveals fishing humor, hard work, intensity, and beauty.

Moore takes a photo of Spit holding a salmon in the air with its fish lips near his lips in a pretend kiss.

The commercial fishing boats travel fast as they move into their districts at the start of the season.

Alaska Native women work their setnets from the shore with skiffs.

8

Jake's crew works hard; the boat loaded full of mounds of salmon.

Jake is asleep in the captain's bunk in the wheelhouse. Moore, Spit, Tana, and Rod slumber in the lower birth, crammed like sardines.

Torden pushes his way to the fishing boundary in front of several boats. The captains raise their fists at him.

Fishing boats line up to deliver fish to the processor boat. Captains smile as they receive a weigh tag. Moore and Spit sing and dance to a hip hop song as they wait.

Nawgek village is bustling as fishermen come in to deliver fish and get supplies.

Grizzly bears sit in the river catching and eating salmon.

Sport fishermen stand in a shallow area of the river competing with bears for salmon.

Exquisitely beautiful colorful salmon swim under the surface of the water, then leap as they swim upstream.

CHAPTER 4
SKATE {RAJIDAE}

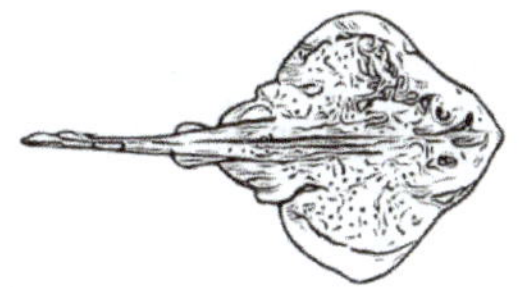

Dramatic mountains and an ominous charcoal-grey sky loom over a two-mile wide and three-quarter-mile deep dark hole in the earth. Richard *call-me-Dick* Hunterson, a pudgy man of moderate stature, wearing a suit and hard hat, talks on the phone. His grim, frowning face squints like a mole in the daylight as he walks along a vertigo-inducing catwalk high above the open pit below.

"What else?" he says impatiently.

"The EPA and Army Corps got the nudge from forty-five. The permit process has begun," Dew Plicitus says, standing looking out of a modern office building window with a view of Denali.

"Brilliant," Dick says slowly in a low, sinister voice, the corner of his mouth turning slightly upward. "Keep up the good work. Break the rock for ten rocks."

"Eye's on the prize."

From under the creaking catwalk, Dick's black-soled shoes step slowly into a mountain cave. Black, dirty fluids flow from the ground below with the loud screeching of blades cutting into the rock. A gold-orange slurry pours in narrow canals from the mine into a holding reservoir. As it travels from the earth, its copper color gets deeper and deeper turning dark orange, then reddish in the filter of the dark clouds.

The bright, orange-red of freshly caught salmon meat is sliced quickly and efficiently in a clean, stark-white processing plant. Busy, happy workers, skilled in their craft, deftly filet salmon after salmon.

Moore talks on his phone as he stands outside a funky fishing bar with a large, colorful mural of the village, fishing boats, and salmon behind him. He wears orange fishing overalls and a blue beanie.

"Hi, sis. Sorry I missed the DC rally. Congratulations! Are you running for president now?"

"Very funny. It's OK. I know wild salmon don't wait for movements."

"Nope. They are a movement."

"True!"

"Where are you?"

"We're at the airport heading home," Tilly, wholesome-pretty, fit, with long black hair and an olive complexion, says as she walks through the Washington DC airport holding hands with her fiance, Liam.

"Here's Liam."

"Hey man, how's the fishing?" Liam, a handsome, athletic young man with short curly hair and sparkling blue eyes, asks.

"It's hard."

"Yup. I remember. How's my uncle treating you?"

"He's hard too."

Liam laughs.

"But thanks for the connection and the job, man. I need to save some money for my clothing business and more sailing."

"You got it. Hang in there. It'll be worth it in the end."

"Will do."

"Here's your sister," Liam hands the phone back over to Tilly.

"Can you make the wedding?" Tilly asks, hopefully.

"Wouldn't miss the Burn or the occasion."

"Great! We're going to honeymoon in Alaska, so don't catch all the salmon."

"Fish and Game met all their release targets you'll be happy to know, but there still may be some savin' to do. Gotta run. We're only here to grab the mail and a quick beer. Miss ya, sis."

"Miss you too. Love you. See you on the playa."

Moore turns to walk back into the bar and sees a large, luxury SUV pulling in front of Rakoff Fisheries across the street. Dick Huntington and Dew Plicitus, in expensive tourist attire, sport fishing vests, and hats, get out of the rig and enter the building.

"Fancy duds for Nawgek," Moore says to himself.

CHAPTER 5
PACIFIC COD {GADUS MACROCEPHALUS}

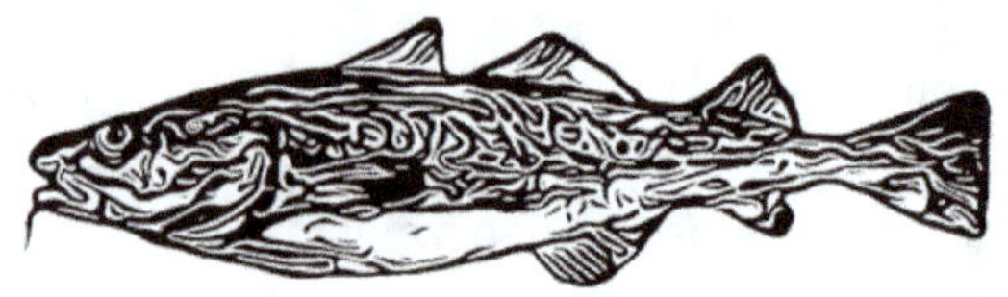

Tied up at Nawgek harbor, Torden works on the main deck as he waits for his crewmen to return after a quick visit to town. Karima, a beautiful Alaska Native young woman with short dark hair, in orange fishing overalls hurries on the dock in front of Torden's boat with a package in her hands. Torden jumps down onto the dock and accidentally bumps into her, knocking the package out of her hands into the water.

"Oh, no!" Karima shouts.

Karima gets on her stomach and tries to reach the package, but the tide takes it out too quickly. Torden quickly climbs back into the boat and grabs a long-handled net. When he returns, the box is too far to reach.

Karima is distressed. "My mother made that for my brother."

Torden takes off his fishing overalls and his shirt. He dives into the water in just his shorts and retrieves the package. He swims back, sets it onto the dock, and climbs out.

"I hope there's something delicious in there," he says, towering over her dripping wet.

"Thank you," Karima says shyly. She quickly rushes past and hands the package to a crewman on the next boat. She turns around and walks past Torden without looking up.

"I'd like a care package," he calls after her.

She stops and turns around, "I don't even know you."

"I'm Torden. Now, you know me."

She continues walking away.

"What boat are you on?"

She doesn't answer.

He calls out, "I rescued your package. You could at least tell me where you fish."

Karima stops. She pauses, thinking, then turns around.

"I set net in Eaglegek."

She turns back around and walks on.

CHAPTER 6
ARTIC COD {BOREOGADUS SARDA}

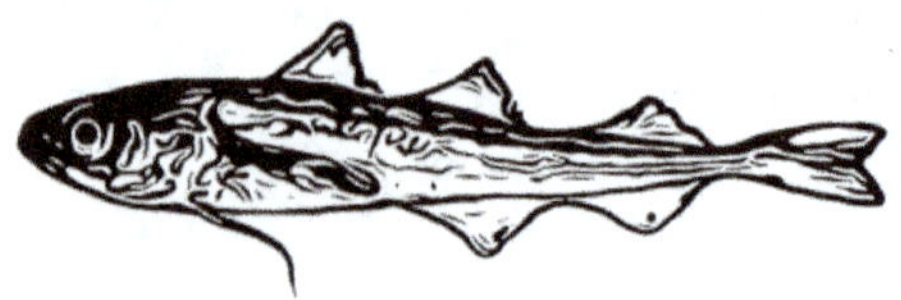

"How's it hittin' over there?" Jake asks.

"It's hot! It might be worth the two-day forced hiatus for you to change districts," Sloane Finnegan, a pretty, spunky redhead in her forties, healthy, with a few well-placed wrinkles from outdoor fishing, says standing at the wheel of her boat holding the radio.

"I'm considering it. Rod says stay and make it pay, but it's crickets over here."

"Heinz is killin' it here too. And not too many hotdogs right now."

"I heard the EPA let the wolves into the henhouse. The permit process has started."

Sloane's head sinks. "You've got to be kidding me." Slowly enunciating each syllable, "Un... fuck... ing... be... lieve... able."

Sloane's eyes widen as she looks back towards her extended net. Her crew gives whoops and hollers.

"Beluga!" Sloane's crewman shouts.

A bright white beluga whale jumps over the net.

"What's going on over there? That many fish?!" Jack asks.

"You won't believe it. A sea canary just jumped my net! I've never seen that before in all my years!"

"Me either. Wow!"

"She's pissed about the goddamn mine too," Sloan says.

Jake shouts to his crew, "Bring her in! We're headed to Eaglegek!"

Rod and Moore work to bring in the net. The crew picks a handful of sparse fish off the net quickly, then tidy the boat as Jake turns and motors off at top speed.

Torden's boat is close to the shore, near a line of set nets in the Eaglegek district.

"What in the world are we doing?!" Lando Lakes, a loud, muscular crewman with dark hair and a ball cap on backward, shouts from the deck below. "We should be out near the boundary, man. There are no fuckin' fish here."

"I'm the captain. I'll decide where we're going."

"You won't make any fans corking these Eskimos' set nets," Lando complains.

"I told you not to use that word, Lakes. They're Yup'ik, Dena'ina or Alutiiq. And since when did you care about our popularity?"

Suddenly, Torden spots Karima working a net in a skiff just off of the shore.

"Where's my care package?" Torden calls out.

"I don't have anything for you. I'm sorry."

Karima's mother looks up from her fishing with a serious look at the other end of the net, near the shore.

"You'll just need to go out with me, then," he calls.

"Come on, man. We're losing the blue cheese, shreddin' the fetti every moment we here!" Lando says, shaking his head angrily.

"I bought you a new truck last year, outside of our deal. We'll make up for it, goddamn it!" Torden softens as he turns to Karima, "What's your number?"

"Shelby at the Trading Post has it if you donate to stop the mine," Karima says with a small smile.

Torden smiles broadly, pleased. He turns the boat around and races off.

Torden's boat races in fast in front of Sloane's boat and net.

"Let her go!!"

The crewmen release the net, and it rolls out in front of Sloane's to cork her.

"You cocky son of a bitch!" she says as she picks up the radio.

"Ixne on the no uckingfay otdogshay."

CHAPTER 7
RED KING CRAB {PARALITHODES CAMTSCHATICUS}

Jake sits at the head of a large table in an old fishing lodge restaurant with his crew, Rod, Moore, Spit, and Tana. Sloane and Heinz, a grizzled fisherman in his sixties, originally from Austria, short with a sturdy build and a weathered face, join them with drinks at the table.

"Here's to the season, the sacred salmon and our friendship," Jake says, holding up his scotch and water.

"Hear hear!" Sloane responds.

The rest of the group raise their glasses. "Cheers!"

"I know we gather after every season, but this one is different," Heinz says with an Austrian accent.

"Yes, it is different," Jake responds.

The group is silent for a few moments, contemplative.

"Maybe we can repurchase the mineral rights from Boreal Extraction," Sloane suggests.

"I knew I should have married you," Heinz says, flirting. "You're rich!"

"No, you know I'm not. I'm just desperate for ideas. The

EPA allowed the permit, and they've put the pedal to the metal to break ground on the mine."

"The bastards," Tana says.

Bart Rakoff, a tall man in his fifties with salt and pepper hair, owner of Rakoff Fisheries, walks up to the table confidently. A waitress arrives with a tray of drinks.

"This gentleman bought you a round of drinks."

"That's a loose use of the term," Heinz says to Sloane under his breath.

"Congratulations on the season, gentlemen, and," looking at Sloane, "beautiful lady."

"Thank you, Bart," Jake responds with a perfunctory smile. "I hear you did well."

"Can't complain," he responds. His wife, Eve, a petite Alaska Native, in her early fifties, pretty with a genuine smile, walks up and stands next to him.

"Eve," Jake says, kissing her hand. "You know this illustrious group," he says with a gesture to the table, "and this is Moore and Spit, my new crewmen."

Spit stands and kisses her hand, copying Jake. The group laughs, and Spit looks confused. Eve is amused. Spit sits back down.

"Smooth, dude," Moore says sarcastically.

"Always," Spit says, smiling.

"Nice to meet you," she says to Moore and Spit. "And I miss all of you," she adds, putting her hands to her heart.

Bart, distracted by others in the room, pulls her away to greet another table. He abruptly turns back around, "Oh, I forgot that I wanted to tell you that we're announcing our price a year in advance. We're paying twenty percent over this year's price. Never too late to come over to Rakoff," he says with a half-smile, then turns and leads Eve to another table. Eve gives the group an apologetic shrug.

"I never understood how such a sweet woman ended up with him," Sloane says.

Amak Nanuk, Bristle Bay Fish and Game Director, a short, stocky, Alaska Native man in his thirties, with a warm, friendly face, drives a small truck down a road along the Kojak River. A large SUV driven by Dew Plicitus tailgates him, driving erratically. Dew speeds up, then slows down, trying to pass. The SUV accelerates to overcome Nanuk's truck on a blind curve and swerves to miss a car driving in the opposite direction, forcing it into a ditch off the road.

Dew speeds up past the scene. "Goddamn Eskimos."

CHAPTER 8
GREENLING {HEXAGRAMMOS}

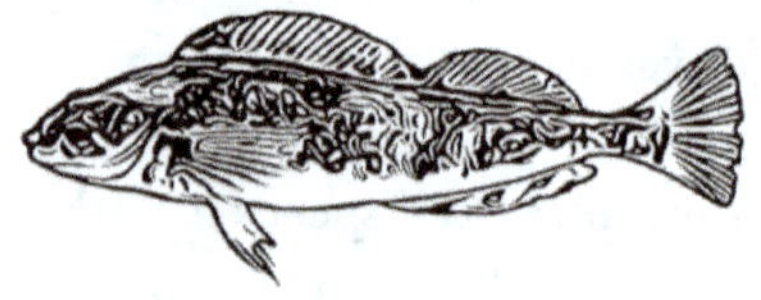

Suddenly, three-quarters of the fishing lodge restaurant guests stand up out of respect as an elderly matron enters the room. Many people say hello. Others wave and smile. Some patrons shake her hand or hold it gently or kiss her on the cheek. Vovo, Jake's grandmother, is delicate with short, white hair, and 106 years old. She wears a handsome short suede jacket, jeans, worn-in but shined Blundstone boots, and a small scarf around her neck. She is vibrant, healthy, and happy from a lifetime and lifestyle of Alaskan salmon.

Vovo holds the arm of her son, Jake's father, Black Selkirk, a distinguished older man in his eighties, as he leads her through the dining room to Jake's table.

Jake stands and leans down to kiss her cheek. "Good evening, Vovo. Hello, Dad," he adds as he shakes Black's hand.

"Where's my goddamn drink?" Black asks. "Move over, son," he says to Spit.

Spit moves over quickly to the next chair, a bit intimidated, and Black sits down in between Moore and Spit, across from Sloane and Heinz. Jake seats Vovo next to him at the head of the table.

"Who was the man who bought the drinks?" Moore asks Jake.

"Benedict Arnold," Heinz says.

"Now, now," Vovo admonishes.

"Sorry, Vovo," Heinz says. "That's the owner of Rakoff Fisheries."

"Seemed stuck up," Spit says, taking a big drink of beer.

"Stuck up is right," Black says is a low gravelly voice, "and greedy."

"We all used to be in business together, Moore," Sloane explains. "He formed a co-op and was one of the first co-ops to share profits with his fisherwomen..." she smiles, "and men. We felt like one big family and became very close. Well, you met Eve. She's an angel and works so hard. We all built up the co-op business over fifteen years. It was a true partnership."

"That sounds great," Spit says.

"Yeah, it was great," Tana continued, "until we heard he'd sold the company for 102 million dollars."

"On the news. Vovo saw it first and texted us," Heinz says.

"Vovo, you text? Right on." Spit says.

Vovo smiles.

"But, that sucks," Spit adds.

"And somehow, he forgot about the whole profit-sharing part of things!" Tana says emotionally.

"Ok. We agreed to put it behind us," Jake says in his deep regal voice.

"Thank you for explaining." Moore pauses, thinking. "Did you say, Rakoff?"

"Yeah. Why?"

"I saw a huge SUV with two guys in Jay-Gatsby-getup going into Rakoff a few weeks ago when we were in town. Brand new fishing duds, first time worn it looked like, and stiff. Two new sparkling Oyster bamboo fly rods on the rig too."

The table is silent.

CHAPTER 9
CAPELIN {OSMERIDAE}

A breeze blows over the river and through a tall tent canopy where groups of people sit at tables filled with beautiful salmon and other local dishes, celebrating the end of the fishing season. The men, women, and children laugh and talk as they serve themselves family style from large platters.

Amak stands and walks to the front of the tent, the river behind him. "We give thanks today..."

The people bow their heads, and some close their eyes.

"... to our ancestors and the Great Spirit for the bounty we receive on this day and have received this season from the salmon who returned once again to these waters. Our path is uncertain in the coming days. There is a darkness that threatens our livelihoods, our culture, and all the beauty that we know. We are strong. We will find the way."

The friends and family nod.

"As my grandfather would say, 'I will love the light for it shows me the way, yet I will endure the darkness because it shows me the stars.' Feast dear friends, and we will find the stars together."

Vovo walks out of the lodge restaurant on Moore's arm with Black and Spit following behind.

Black turns to Moore and Spit. "You two should see Alaska before you go home."

"We plan to, sir."

"Good," says Vovo. "You are smart boys."

"Hope to see you next season," Black says.

Moore and Spit shake Black's hand.

Vovo hugs the boys. "If you need any work for the rest of the summer, just let us know. We have lots of projects on the ranch and fishing guests to tend to."

"Thanks again," Moore responds.

"Where's your rig?" Vovo asks, looking at the parking lot.

"I think we're going to stay for one more beer," Moore says.

"Oh, to be young!" Vovo sighs.

Moore and Spit walk up to the bar and sit next to Tana. Torden is at the opposite end of the bar talking loudly, drinking, dancing, and singing with Lando and Six, a young black crewman with a sixth finger on his left hand. Lando pushes buttons on the jukebox, and the hip hop song *I'm on a Boat* plays loudly. They sing along.

"Hey, you guys do OK with the old geezer's boat?" Lando shouts over the music, his speech a bit slurred.

"Huh?" Spit grunts.

"Did you make any money, surf-boy?"

Spit looks confused.

Tana jumps in. "We did fine, thanks," she says, dryly.

"We saw you out there in the crowd getting pushed

around," Torden says, puffing out his chest. He raps to the rhythm of the song, mimicking a hip hop artist with hand gestures. "We can't be bothered. We fish the limits. We push the limits. We're the fastest on the bay."

"Sounds good, man. Fish on," Moore says, drinking his beer, turning away.

"You two don't look like you're cut out for this tough work," Torden continues relentlessly.

"Right on," Spit says. "I like girls and ganja, man, and there wasn't any of that on the boat."

Six laughs and smiles warmly. Torden and Lando laugh. They point at Spit, rudely, whispering to themselves.

"Well, if the job description is being an asshole, then maybe not," Moore says.

Tana laughs and stands up. "Let's get outta here, guys."

Moore and Spit down their beer, and the three walk out.

CHAPTER 10
POACHER {AGONIDAE}

Vovo stands at the back door of a large fishing lodge on the river. Spit pulls up in a well-maintained 1979 Scout SUV with Moore in the passenger seat.

"The Johnson group arrives at 2:00 pm. Pull the Scout in between those trees, so they have room to unload."

"Yes, ma'am," Spit answers.

Spit attempts to parallel park. He pulls in and misses the mark. He pulls out and retries, missing again.

Vovo walks over. "Are you telling me no one has ever taught you to parallel park, young man?"

"No, Vovo. I guess not," Spit responds, sheepishly.

"OK. Pull out. Let's start from scratch."

Spit pulls out in front of the space.

"With anything you learn, you need a goal to visualize."

"OK."

"Have you seen The Italian Job?"

"Yep," Spencer answers, smiling.

Moore nods.

"Visualize this classic rig sliding right into place like those

Minis with only an inch in front and back. Go on. Close your eyes."

The boys close their eyes.

"OK, now you'll need your eyes open to drive."

Spit and Moore open their eyes.

"All you need to remember is that your back right wheel's last resting place is right where you're going to put it now, as the first step. Point it in towards the imaginary curb. Don't be shy, but don't hit the tree!"

Spit backs in slowly.

"Stop... Stop there, just before that wheel hits the curb."

Spit places the right back wheel in position, smiling proudly.

"Now, turn your wheel sharply to the left to roll in the front end of the rig."

Spit follows her direction.

"That's right. There you go."

He rolls it into place perfectly between the trees.

"Brilliant!"

"Thanks, Vovo!"

"Now, unload the supplies and get the fishing boat ready for the guests."

"Yes, ma'am." They say in unison.

"Tonight, we'll practice on the tundra. Bring my 'juana, please."

Bright orange cones mark the bare tundra, a vast gravelly area with low moss-like grasses. From a distance, Vovo speeds behind the wheel of a Jeep with a roll bar. She adeptly pulls in between the cones like an Italian Job movie stunt driver. Spit in the Scout and Moore in a small beat-up pickup truck, laugh and let out loud whoops as they practice on their designated tundra runways, pulling their rigs in fast and skillfully.

Spit sits on the top of the Scout, his back resting on the windshield. Moore and Vovo pick salmonberries and place them in a small bowl. Vovo hands the bowl to Spit as Moore lifts her easily up onto the hood of the Scout. She scoots over next to Spit. Moore climbs up after her.

The three rest on the windshield of the rig overlooking the beautiful Alaskan countryside with an immense, blue sky above them. Spit lights a small pipe and passes it to Vovo, who takes a hit. She gives the boys a thumbs up, holding her breath.

Vovo holds the bowl of bright cloudberries. Moore and Spit alternate reaching over for a berry as they all look out over the tundra.

CHAPTER 11
STELLER SEA LION
{EUMETOPIAS JUBATUS}

Karima stands behind Torden on his boat as it races up the river. She smiles as the wind rushes through her short hair. They wear orange fishing overalls. Torden steers the vessel in a weaving pattern to avoid low spots.

"I don't see any fish," Torden says, frustrated.

"They're over there," Karima motions with a nod.

"Where?" Torden looks at her quizzically.

"There," Karima points. "I don't think you can get there. It's too shallow. But if you could, they're over there."

Torden accelerates to full speed and hydroplanes over the low area and arrives at the spot where Karima pointed.

"Take the wheel!"

He runs down to the back and releases the net as Karima steers the boat for a few minutes. Fish jump out of the water as the net rolls out.

"Well, I'll be damned. How did you see those?"

"I don't see them, silly. I feel them." She puts her hand on her heart.

"Well, it worked!" He shakes his head.

The two get to know each other over the hours that follow. They talk about each other's families as the net is out filling with salmon. Torden reels in the net, and the two of them work together, pulling the fish off, talking and laughing. Torden steps away to answer a call, and Karima throws a fish at him, playfully. They deliver fish to a processor boat. Torden receives the weigh tag, and the two of them shake hands, smiling. As the sun sets, they stand together at the wheel, riding fast along the water.

Torden and Karima sit next to each other under the night sky. A bottle of wine and glasses are on the boat's console along with bread, cheese, and smoked salmon.

"Thanks for coming on a date with me," Torden says.

"I wouldn't call twelve hours of fishing a date," Karima teases.

"The guys went home for the season. I always like to work for another week. It's not a whole lot of money, but it's peaceful."

"I can see why you like it," she says, looking out over the water.

"Why did you decide to come?"

"The truth is that you are the first man who asked me what boat I was on and didn't just assume that I set net."

"Hmmm. Seems natural to me. What's your best memory of fishing?"

Karima closes her eyes. She opens them. "A few years ago, I saw the most amazing sight. It was peak season, and one evening when the sun was low in the sky, and my mom and I waited in anticipation for the hour of fishing to start, the sun shone through the waves, and we could see the salmon coming right at us. Thousands upon thousands riding the waves. The sparkling blue water and sunset's glowing warm light on the red beauty of the salmon were magical."

Torden smiled as she finished her story.

"Hey, look at those lights over there," Torden says, surprised.

On the coast, they see about twenty small flashing lights, beautiful below the stars in the night sky.

"Some people are bringing back some old customs in the hope it will drive away the evil mine."

"What are they saying?"

Karima looks at the lights. "They're chanting. The lights are old lanterns with a mirror to call the aurora borealis, which we believe represents the animal spirits, including the salmon. They chant for the return of the salmon spirit to fight the mine."

"Can you communicate with them?"

"I've learned some of it. Yes."

"I have a flashlight and a mirror." Torden jumps up excitedly to get them, then hands them to Karima.

"You're silly." She laughs. "I'll shine it downward. I don't think it's fair to call all the salmon to you. You've caught enough!" she teases.

Karima takes the light, puts the mirror over it, then takes the mirror off, making a rhythmic pattern onto the wine in Torden's glass.

"Very pretty. What did you say?"

"Thunder."

He is surprised. "Show me again," he requests softly.

She repeats the light pattern slowly. Then she looks at him. Torden turns the flashlight off, leans in, and they kiss for the first time as the lights blink along the shore in the distance.

CHAPTER 12
GIANT SEA STAR {EVASTERIAS ECHINOSOMA}

Moore, Tilly, and Pedro, Tilly's black, curly-haired water dog, sit in a small fishing boat on the Kojak river. They wear fishing gear and mesh hoods.

"I'm taking this thing off," Tilly says.

"Good luck. The mosquito is the state bird of Alaska."

Tilly swats her face. She laughs and quickly puts the hood back on. "You're right!"

Moore pulls a hand-tied fly out of his vintage wicker tackle box and ties it to Tilly's line.

"I'm observing you to learn. It's so peaceful out here. I might need to take up the hobby."

"Fishing might be too slow for you, sis. And, it's an art, not a hobby."

"I stand corrected," Tilly smiles, enjoying seeing her brother in his element.

Moore stands. "OK, this flat-bottom boat is pretty steady, but take your time getting up."

Tilly stands, a little wobbly.

"Fly fishing is like a song."

"A song?"

"Yes, it has a rhythm and a tempo. You move the rod back and forth from 10 to 1 o'clock through a ninety-degree angle at a gentle speed," Moore demonstrates, "... slowly unrolling the line."

"OK." Tilly watches intently.

"I like to count 'one-two' taking it back and 'three-four' bringing it forward. Or for you, 'take time'... 'to breathe.'"

Tilly laughs. "Sounds easy. Can I watch first?"

Moore takes the rod, and with graceful, artful motions moves it back and forth, back and forth, then casts with skill into a shadowed area of the river.

Moore brings in the line, then hands Tilly the rod and stands behind her, holding her arm to make the motions back and forth. Pedro's head moves side to side following the rod.

"One more important thing is to avoid the hook. You don't want it in your head or Pedro's cheek or my ass."

"OK!"

Moore lets go. Tilly continues moving the rod back and forth and back and forth. She releases, and the line goes straight down just a few feet from the boat. Pedro barks.

"Shucks. You make it look so easy."

"You'll get it," Moore smiles.

Tilly keeps practicing, improving with each cast. The breeze makes waves through her long hair, and the curving strands match the curling, floating line in the air.

"Leave your line in the water. Let's sit and have a bite."

Moore unpacks two sandwiches and hands Pedro a treat.

"Have you enjoyed fishing and working for Vovo?" Tilly asks.

"It's amazing. I've never seen a sky like this or the power of fifty million salmon swimming past in a period of just a few weeks. They say that God made Bristle Bay for salmon."

"Wow."

"Till, remember in Hawaii when you asked for my help?"

"Of course. I'm still so grateful for you and Spit."

"We need your help now."

"What is it?"

"I know you're in the middle of your honeymoon and everything, but the salmon are in trouble. Not just the salmon but the livelihood and culture of the Native people." Moore gets more passionate as he speaks. "A huge mining company, Boreal Extraction, just announced it's going to break ground on a mine just above Bristle Bay to get at the largest deposit of gold and copper in the world."

"Heavens, no."

"They have cloaked messages. To the community, they downplay the size and timing of the mine, saying they plan only to mine twelve percent and finish in twenty years. To investors, they say it's a 100-year project. They defeated the mine many times before, and people thought it was over, but Boreal Extraction isn't afraid of controversy. That, coupled with POTUS who's turning over our natural park treasures to mining, has allowed them to slip back in. They're in permitting and expected to break ground next spring or summer."

"Who's running it?"

Moore raises his voice. "A guy named Richard Hunterson. You can call him Dick. The bastard is greed personified. Vovo read a quote to me. I don't remember the exact wording, but basically, the Dick said what got him hooked on making money from natural resources was that the business takes something where there was nothing, invests a little in it, and it's worth ten or a hundred times more."

"That's so typical. The evaluation of nature as nothing."

"And they've also hired an experienced lobbyist who will get $10 million if he gets the mine started."

"Oh, my," Tilly says, concerned.

"I just can't fathom the aftermath of the mine contamination. The death of the salmon."

Moore puts his head in his hands, and Tilly sees tears fall onto the floor of the boat. She puts her hand on his shoulder. They sit quietly.

The line suddenly moves. Tilly squeals.

"You've got one!" Moore says, wiping his eyes.

Moore helps her reel it in. "Take it slow, so we don't hurt it."

"How can I help?"

"The governor doesn't seem to be doing anything. I thought you could go see her."

"I don't know what I will say to her, but yes, I can try."

Tilly pulls the fish out of the water. "It's so pretty!"

Moore snaps a picture of Tilly holding the fish with Pedro. Pedro gets excited and wants to play with the jiggling fish. Tilly loses her balance and falls in the water. Pedro leaps in after her. She comes up laughing.

"Next time we'll wade," Moore says.

They laugh as Moore pulls her back into the boat.

CHAPTER 13

CHUM SALMON
{ONCORHYMCHUS KETA}

"Heinz, can you meet me in San Francisco next Wednesday?" Sloane says into her phone, standing near a one-room ramshackle office for a puddle jumper commuter plane. She wears well-worn Red Ants Pants, a denim long-sleeve shirt with a tank top underneath, aviator sunglasses, and a ball cap that says *Girls Fish*.

"I just got home from two months of fishing. My wife will kill me."

"It's important. I have a lead on the mine, but I need a bulldog Austrian with me."

"What's it about?"

A small plane lands on a short runway and taxies up to the office. The propeller noise is loud, and Sloane puts her finger in her ear.

"My plane home just landed. Gotta run!" she shouts.

"Send me the details."

"I'll pick you up at the airport!"

Sloane and Heinz sit in the back of an Uber sedan traveling over the Bay Bridge towards San Francisco with a view of the Golden Gate in the distance. Sloane is elegant in a simple royal blue, fitted dress and high heels, her styled red hair in gentle waves, a stark contrast to her fishing life. Heinz looks rugged but cleaned up, wearing an Orvis canvas barn coat with a brown corduroy collar and a red shirt.

"Where are we headed?"

"Remember, I told you guys that we should buy the mine's mineral rights?"

"Yes."

"Turns out there were a whole lot of fishermen who never signed up for the class action price-fixing suit or died in the middle of it. The market crashed during that time, so some folks were just trying to make ends meet and missed it."

"I was just getting started, still renting my boat. But how does it relate to the mine?"

"I'm not sure yet, but I thought the attorney who handled the case might help us squeeze more money out of the old lawsuit to fight the mine."

Tilly and Liam paddle in a two-person kayak on the river. Tilly phones Frida, a long-time family friend and spiritual guide. Frida is pretty with deep set wrinkles on her face and long grey hair. She stands on the edge of Lake Bijou Nez, tall pine trees surrounding her.

"Hello, dear one."

"Frida, I need your help."

"What is it?"

"Can you come to Nawgek tomorrow?"

"Of course, anything for you. How can I get there by tomorrow?"

"Camas will bring you the tickets and drive you to the airport. I'll explain when I see you."

CHAPTER 14
SAND LACE {AMMODYTES HEXAPTERUS}

Chalky Michigan, an older man in his eighties with curly grey hair, walks out of his office to the waiting room with an unlit cigar in his hand. He greets Sloane and Heinz and leads them into his office with a view of Nob Hill and the San Francisco Bay.

Chalky motions for them to sit. "How can I help you today," he says in a smooth baritone.

"I'm Sloane. This is Heinz. We own commercial fishing boats in Bristle Bay."

"Bristle Bay! The Grand Canyon of salmon."

"Yes, it is, sir," Sloane responds.

"You represented the Bristle Bay fisherman in the price-fixing class action, right?" Heinz asks, pointedly.

"Yes, Heinz. You're no spring chicken. Were you in the suit?"

"I was, yes. I retired on my 2,127 dollars and 66 cents. What did you do with your sixteen million?"

"You're here to complain about the outcome after twenty years?"

"Of course not, sir," Sloane says, sweetly. "I know your

record as a modern-day Robin Hood, helping the little guy, and we need your help."

Chalky smiles at her, enjoying the flattery. "Call me Chalky. What can I do?"

"We know a fisherman who died before he could file a claim. Also, there were 4,500 claims out of 8,000 fisherman."

"That sounds about right."

"We're wondering if any of those fisherman might still have a claim."

"I'm sorry, lassie. The statute of limitations has passed."

"Oh," Sloane says, disappointed.

"What were you hoping to accomplish?" Chalky asks.

"Copper Cobra mine has told investors they're breaking ground next June. I know it may sound far-fetched, but we were trying to find a way to buy them out."

"Darlin', they estimate those minerals to be worth $500 billion, give or take a few billion."

"Oro Sangriente backed out because they said they thought the mine didn't have a chance. Maybe it's not worth that much," Sloane says, hopefully.

"Her name is Sloane, not darlin', and she is one of the top fishermen... fisherwomen... in Bristle Bay," Heinz adds. "If you are a true Robin Hood, as you say..."

"I've slowed down," Chalky admits.

"Be that as it may, if you're the Joe Frazier of the legal world, pugnacious, Chalky "Cockey" Michigan, then why don't you genuinely do some good?" Heinz asks firmly.

"I've done good. I pull for the underdog every single time."

"Chalky," Sloane continues sweetly, "We came here because we need help, and everyone tells us that besides being a lawyer, you also know business, and you've worked for the little guy your entire life."

"Let me let this simmer," Chalky says, looking sternly at

Heinz. He turns to Sloane. "I might have an idea or two. Maybe I can get the Japanese involved. They've been bullish on salmon since the Norwegians sold them on it." He smiles at Sloane and stands up.

"Thank you for seeing us," Sloane says.

"Thank you," Heinz says, holding out his hand.

Chalky shakes his hand firmly, then kisses Sloane on the cheek. Sloane and Heinz walk out of the office.

"You have him wrapped around your finger, good cop."

"Not sure about that, but he's well-connected." Sloane swings her curvy hips in an exaggerated sexy swagger as they walk down the office hall.

CHAPTER 15
SCULPIN {COTTODEA}

Tilly and Frida flow in vinyasa yoga poses at the top of a hill overlooking Bristle Bay. Fishermen and women with their set nets at regular intervals work along the shore. Frida and Tilly sit and begin to chant. The sound carries to the shore, and an Alaska Native woman with a baby in a backpack turns her face to listen to the beautiful sounds.

"The Native people are being influenced by the mine. One group of people was granted shares of the mine and are being fed promises of money and jobs. Greed, the white man's whiskey, is subtly seeping into their minds, just like the acid runoff that will kill the salmon. It's intoxicating, and it's capturing some of them, I fear." Tilly pleads, "I need your help to wake them up from an illusion of riches."

"Let us pray to our ancestors."

Tilly closes her eyes. "Yes."

They face each other, holding hands lightly.

"Great Spirits of the air, water, earth, and fire, as we sit in your presence, you remind us that many years before, Raven traveled by canoe from the river to the salmon people's village."

Tilly chants softly as Frida recounts the ancient tale.

"The chief invited Raven for dinner but warned him not to eat any of the bones of the salmon. Raven was mischievous and hid a bone in his mouth."

Dew Plicitus meets with a Native group, smiling, shaking hands, showing them papers with figures.

"After dinner, when the chief threw the bones into the river, they turned into salmon, but the people knew something was wrong."

Tilly's chanting continues.

"Raven reluctantly returned the missing bone, and the fish transformed into the chief's daughter. Raven grabbed the girl, taking her away in his canoe."

Tilly is silent.

"Wise spirits, when Raven returns next year with the sacred salmon, to release her..."

Far up the Kojack river, in a large lake of spawning salmon, a black raven flies over.

"We ask that you allow him to fulfill his promise to release the salmon back to its people."

Frida and Tilly bow their heads, almost touching.

Tilly and Liam walk with Pedro along the shoreline near the oldest fish processing plant in Nawgek, a wood warehouse structure with tall industrial spaces and ancient signage. Tilly's best friend, Camas, a strong young woman in her twenties, with curly strawberry blond hair, freckles, a fit full-figure and one arm decorated in artistic tattoos, sits at Heaven's Brother's in Sandglass and answers her phone.

"Cam, I have to stay in Alaska."

"What the frigid?!"

"I know, I know. I told you I'd be home Saturday."

"Yes, and that you'd be back in the saddle helping with your growing One More Year organization."

"I need your help."

"Go," she says, exasperated.

"I need you to research gold and copper mining."

"Are you inheriting a mine?"

"In a way. We're inheriting it, but we're not getting rich."

"Damn. How am I going to get rich? Josh isn't rich, either."

"You're rich in love, remember? Let me know what you find!"

CHAPTER 16
FLATFISH {PLEURONECTIDAE}

Camas gets out of the shower and pulls a towel around her voluptuous body, then a towel on her head. She sits down on her bed in front of a large picture window with beautiful orange, red and yellow leaves falling and large piles of colorful leaves covering the streets. She calls Tilly.

"Listen to this," Camas says.

"Listening."

"I have an EPA report with the dangers of accidental runoff and spills related to mining. At least 27 out of 52 states are represented, and many states have multiple disasters."

"Wow. Will you send that to me, please?"

"I also have a list of mining chemical spills from 1990 to 2019. It's pretty fucking depressing."

"I was worried about that."

Camas looks up and sees a man looking at her from the street. She pauses, thinking.

"Hey, I'm in my towel with my blinds up, and some guy on the street is watching me, and it just gave me an awesome idea!"

"An idea to close your blinds, perhaps?!"

"Nope..." She smiles and waves at the man on the street. "... but it could bring attention to these spills."

"What's your idea?"

"Let me pull it together, and I'll send it to you."

"Cam, we don't have much time."

"I know, sista."

Spit cleans a lodge room, pulling sheets off of the bed and changing it. "Hey man, I thought we'd be taking the fishing boats out. Hobnobbin' with celebrities."

Moore scrubs the bathroom toilet, "Step up or down from fish guts?"

"Up. There's spinach here."

"See, you're moving up."

The door opens, and Dew enters, talking on his phone. Moore tries to catch his eye, motioning towards the door to ask if they should leave for his privacy. Dew dismisses him with a mean stare and a wave of his hand.

Moore and Spit continue cleaning.

"No, no, it's OK. I know we seem light on start-up capital. Ko will step up with the funds when it's time."

Dew grabs something from his desk and walks out of the room.

The guys gather their cleaning supplies on a cart to leave.

"Sparkly clean," Spit says, running his hands over the smooth bedspread with a flamboyant flourish.

"Please tip your housemaid," Moore says in falsetto as he puts the tip envelope on the desk. They lock arms and curtesy in front of the mirror and walk out.

CHAPTER 17

YELLOW FIN SOLE {LIMANDA ASPERA}

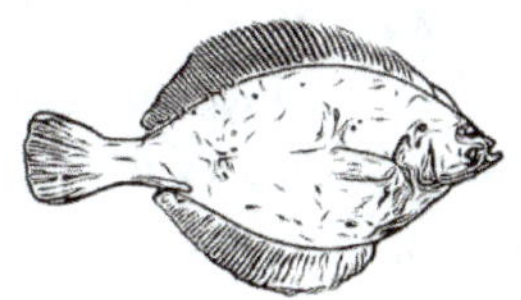

Liam is at the kitchen counter of Vovo's lodge drinking a coffee. Tilly is on her laptop at the kitchen table.

"My love, come see this," Tilly says to Liam.

"What is it?"

"It's something from Camas. She wants us to watch it together."

Liam walks over and leans down to look over Tilly's shoulder.

Tilly reads aloud, "She says, *Follow my instructions, gal pal Till. One: Read the press release below. Two: watch the videos.*"

Vovo walks into the kitchen and sits across from Tilly at the table. Liam pours Vovo a cup of coffee, brings it to her, and kisses her on the cheek. She squeezes his hand for a moment, releases it, and Liam returns to Tilly's side.

Tilly continues reading, "For immediate release, a young Sandglass woman who is the CFO of the environmental organization One More Year, wants you to know that you should send the EPA and your congressman a message and all of your friends to stop the Copper Cobra mine in Bristle Bay, Alaska.

In order to remind everyone of the incredible dangers, Camas will read once a day until the mine is defeated. She is going to read from reports from the EPA of horrific spills. Just the type of thing that can happen to kill the largest sockeye salmon run in the world if we don't stop it. If you're worried it will be boring, you don't know Camas. Please watch her first episodes here. Choose your video based on the following: Click here if you want to see sexy Camas (PG13-rated). Click here if you want your kids to watch it too (G-rated). Click here if you want to get mad with Camas (R-rated)."

"Get's your attention, that's for sure," Liam says.

"That's my Cam," Tilly agrees. "What should we pick first?"

"Get mad with Camas!" Vovo calls out.

Tilly smiles and clicks on the video. Vovo walks over and sits next to Tilly at the table.

The video launches and Camas appears on the screen wearing a low cut top with her voluptuous cleavage revealed.

Camas speaks loudly over heavy metal music in the background. "Welcome to your daily episode of Kill Cobra. Let's get fuckin' mad today as I read real dangers from real mines in a real EPA report. There is a link to the report under this video. Let's rock!"

Camas speaks loudly and quickly. "Iron Mountain Mine. Quote, uncontrolled release kills 200,000 salmon, unquote. That's right! 200,000 goddamn beautiful salmon. Here's what the fuckin' morons did at Iron Mountain mine in Californi-eye-ay. They dropped the fuckin' ball. Quote, acid mine drainage was created by the infiltration of rainwater and the migration of groundwater through the massive sulfide mineral zone, unquote. That means things that happen everyday... duh, fuckin' rain and water in the earth passed through their toxic shit. Let's continue. Quote, as the water passed through the ore... that's the same shit they're planning to dig up at

Cobra, by the way, sulfuric acid was produced, unquote. Acid, that's just fuckin' unbelievable. If you didn't already know, acid is the nasty byproduct of mining and not the fun thing you and I do to rave out. Onward! Quote, copper, zinc, and cadmium were leached from the mineralized zone by the acidic water."

Camas continues, more animated, and rockin' to the music. "The acid mine drainage was eventually discharged through mine exits or by groundwater seepage into streams in the Spring Creek watershed, unquote. Oh, fuck! Quote, in general, acid mine drainage generation was seasonal and was accelerated during periods of heavy rainfall, unquote."

The loud rock music continues as Camas leans forward and pushes her arms together to make her cleavage more pronounced. "Duh, they are saying as the weather gets nasty, there's more water. Note to self; if the bastards try to say technology in safety has improved after I told them to shove the mine up their ass, I would say that climate events are going to wreak havoc everywhere, and there's no way in hell, they can control the fucky muck. My good friends, if you're not already puking your guts, there's more. Quote, surface water pollution resulted in heavy metal bioaccumulation in fish, unquote. That means the fish were glowing neon green, like an all-night rave party. Quote, and contamination of the Sacramento River, Redding's drinking water supply, where was Erin Brokovich when you needed her, as a result of surface water and groundwater discharges, Slickrock Creek, Boulder Creek, and Flat Creek were devoid of aquatic life..."

She gets louder, "Unquote! Devoid means every swimming thing was a big X-on-eyeballs dead! Oh, wait! Don't go. There's more! Quote, In addition, heavy rains caused uncontrolled releases of contaminated water from Spring Creek Reservoir, which killed approximately 200,000 salmon. Acid mine drainage from the mine was one cause of a drastic decline in King Salmon as well, unquote. There you have it. And by the way, your pointer finger is the sockeye salmon. It can 'sock' your eye out."

Camas dips her index finger into red food coloring, and it comes out red. She dries it off and raises her red finger to the sky, then pops it up to make a jumping salmon motion. "Raise it red!!"

The heavy metal music gets louder.

"Tune in tomorrow for your next earth-shaking *mine*-fucked experience with Camas. Rock on!"

Camas bangs her head in the air to the music. Her red finger points to the sky and makes sockeye salmon jumps in the air.

The music fades out. Tilly, Liam and Vovo look at one another.

Vovo raises both hands in the air, one with a pointed finger, "Raise it red!"

CHAPTER 18
SHRIMP {CRANGONIDAE}

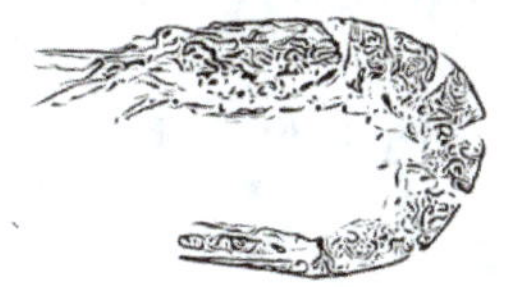

Joyful, playful pop music plays as a bright red index finger points to a goldfish swimming in a bowl. Camas sits in a tiny sailboat on Lake Bijou Nez in shallow water near the beach. She is extra cute with her curly strawberry blond hair in side ponytails, in a sexy sailor outfit holding the goldfish bowl. Camas' boyfriend, Josh, an athletic, young black man in his late twenties, with a short beard, maneuvers the boat with a rudder at the stern. He wears a Captain's hat and films Camas with his phone in one hand as they sail in a very slow circle.

"Hi kids, I'm your Aunt Camas," she says in a lilting, teacher-like voice, "and I want to let you know that mines are bad and fish are good. How do I know that? Well, this lake is full of fish, and this bowl is full of one fish, my fish *Smoothie*. I named it that because, well, I love smoothies. Smoothie's a very happy fish. The fish in this lake are also happy. Aren't they, Captain Josh?"

Josh turns the phone around to film himself, "Very happy, Aunt Camas!" Josh exclaims, the boat rocking when he shouts.

"Thank you, Captain Josh, don't rock the boat. We'll rock the boat later on," Camas says, winking at Josh.

"Kids, what do the fish in this lake and the fish in the bowl need to be happy and healthy?"

Tilly and Camas's good friends, Ike and The Bike Guys, Cutter, Joe, and Reeve stand chest-deep in the water. A group of young kids plays behind them on the beach.

"Food?!" shouts Cutter, 6'2" in his early thirties with red hair and a beard, with a little boy voice and his hat on backward.

"That's right! Thank you, young man. What else?" Camas asks.

Reeve, a handsome man in his late forties with salt and pepper hair, riding a blow-up sea horse, shouts, "Oxygen?" in a little boy falsetto.

"Yes! Fish need oxygen that they breathe under the water. What else do fish need? Anyone?"

Ike, an older man, grey-bearded, with tan leathery skin, wearing a small sailor's hat, calls out in a deep voice, "Clean water, Aunt Camas?"

"Bingo, uncle Ike. Clean water!"

"Hey, Joe, what would happen if the fish didn't have clean water?" Ike asks.

"You mean if something bad got into their water, Ike?" Joe says dramatically.

Joe walks to the sailboat and dumps red food coloring into the goldfish bowl. Ike and the Bike Guys gasp in unison with wide eyes.

"This food coloring doesn't harm this goldfish, but there are chemicals from mining that get into water like this and hurt the fish. And those chemicals are very bad and can't be taken out. They make the fish like Smoothie die. Fish including all five species of Pacific salmon..."

She points to each of her fingers, beginning with her

thumb, "Chum, sockeye, king, silver, and pink. And rainbow trout, arctic char, grayling, northern pike, lake trout, and Dolly Varden."

"Dolly Parton?" Ike asks, playfully.

Camas laughs. "No, Ike. Dolly Varden."

"That's a lot of fish," Josh adds. "Not to mention other sea life, like seals and whales."

"What can we do, Aunt Camas?" Ike and the Bike Guys ask in unison.

"Tell your mom and dad and anyone you know that mining is bad for goldfish. Will you do that for me?"

The four guys jump high out of the water and high five, "Yes!" And come down, and their splashes get Camas and Josh all wet.

"And ask your mom to buy you some red food coloring so you can paint your finger like a sockeye red, just like me! Just dip it in and hold!"

Josh and the other guys hold their index fingers in the fishbowl.

"Then raise it red!" She says, pointing her finger to the sky.

"See you next time. Save the fish! Love you!"

Camas makes a heart with her two hands at her sternum, then points her red index finger up and smiles at the camera.

Moore, Spit, and Vovo stand in the driveway in front of the lodge. Black stands by the Scout, waiting to drive them to the airport.

"Vovo, thanks for letting us stay for the summer and for the job," Moore says

"Yeah, thanks for the dough, Vovo," Spit adds. He smiles, pleased he has made a rhyme.

"You've got the rhythm and the rhyme, young men," Vovo says, making hip hop hands.

They hug her.

"Where are you off to?" Black asks.

"We have a lead on something with the mine. We're headed to Vancouver to see what we can find out."

"Those are my boys! When you're out chasing clues, chase some skirts too. I made a rhyme!"

"Fer sure!" Spit says.

The boys hug Vovo again, jump into the Scout with Black, and wave to Vovo as they drive away.

CHAPTER 19
KING SALMON
{ONCHORHYNCHUS
TSHAWYTSCHA}

Camas sits at an elaborate dinner table with candles, wine, and a beautiful salmon filet on her plate, wearing a long, sexy, evening dress. Her dress has a long slit in the side, showing a lot of her leg, and is low cut exposing her bountiful cleavage. Sultry music plays as the snow falls outside and rests on the window ledge and the shore of Lake Bijou Nez.

Camas speaks very low, slowly and seductively. "Hello, and welcome to Sexy Salmon with Camas. You know, sometimes, there are obvious comparisons that just can't be ignored, such as my likeness to some of the sexiest women in history. I've been compared many times to," making alluring expressions and sexy poses at each name, "Cleopatra, Brigit Bardot, Tina Turner, Amy Schumer, Marilyn Monroe, and Ginger on Gilligan's Island."

She takes a slow drink of wine. "A similar comparison is the Bingham Kennecott mine to the horrific Copper Cobra mine. These two mines are said to be comparable, except that Cobra will be larger. In this scenario, size really does matter."

Slowly and seductively, she whispers, "Close your door and

listen closely, as I tell you something very, very.... very sexy. Are you listening? According to environmental specialists, the mine has had adverse environmental effects on the habitats of fish and wild animals as well as air and water pollution, creating health hazards to the surrounding public. Like what you may ask?"

Striptease music plays as she reads the list. "1999. 100 million gallons of arsenic water, cause of leak unknown. 2004. Four million gallons of arsenic water. Cracked pipe." Her voice is breathier and builds with intensity. "2000. Five million gallons of sulfuric acid. Flange failure."

Camas's voice climbs from seductive to a loud climax, "My lovelies, there are multiple spills per year with the words: clogged, ruptured," her voice quickens, "malfunctioned, leaked, cracked!"

She lets out a heaving sigh and continues in her sexy voice, "More tomorrow. There are many more spills from this twin mine. The EPA has estimated a 72-square-mile plume of contaminated groundwater due to these spills. Remember how I mentioned that Bingham resembles Copper Cobra? 72 miles from Cobra is the mouth of Bristle Bay. Let's dine, my loves!"

Camas takes a sip of wine, then picks up a bit of salmon on her fork and slowly puts it into her mouth, looking into the camera. She spits it out violently, and it shoots across the table.

"I miss the old salmon that didn't taste like a car battery," she says forlornly. "Tune in tomorrow for more sexy salmon with Camas. And remember..." She moves her red index finger slowly over her slightly open lip-glossed lower lip, turning her head seductively. Then she points her finger straight at the camera with a sexy smile.

"Raise it red!"

CHAPTER 20

WALRUS {ODOBENUS ROSMARUS}

Moore and Spit drink coffee at a Vancouver café filled with artistic boho types, stylish techies, and nerdy bookworms. Moore draws a clothing design in his sketchbook. Spit has headphones on and reads a graphic novel.

Spit looks up. "Are you nervous about the new job? You're not really an engineer."

"I think it'll be OK."

"What are you looking for when you're in there?"

"I have no idea."

"What are you going to do tomorrow when I'm at work?" Moore asks Spit.

"I have no idea."

Amak drives an ATV through the tundra, then along backwoods trails along Iliana Lake near the proposed mine site. He gets off of the vehicle and walks through the woods, where he finds an area of surveyed land with yellow-ribboned stakes. He walks for a few miles from stake to stake. The perimeter is diverse, beautiful, and vast. He stops, sits, and takes a drink from his water bottle, overlooking the lake. Amak looks to his left, and twenty yards away, an immense Grizzly bear sits eating. They look at each other calmly.

Dick lies face down on a massage table. He holds his cell phone as a masseuse massages his pudgy body and hairy back.

"Get the fuckin' Natives on board. Get the goddamn yahoo fishermen on board too for that million a year I pay you!" Dick commands.

Dew sits across from Bart in Bart's offices on the phone. "Ko's donation to the Natives is working out well. They sold their shares, but have put up a mining website with positive information. They call it neutral, but it's doing its job. They all got a nice payout. Behind the scenes, they're being told it's an example of future rewards... jobs and other side payouts. Some of the money is training the indigenous in engineering and geology. Nice to work at a mine in your backyard. We paid Rakoff to bring fishermen on board. If they come over to Bart, they get a huge raise and our company stock."

Bart nods and gives a thumbs up.

"It better work, DP. I'm cutting off my right nut to pay you when this mine is split open."

CHAPTER 21

ALASKA PLAICE {PLEURONECTES QUADRITUBERCALATUS}

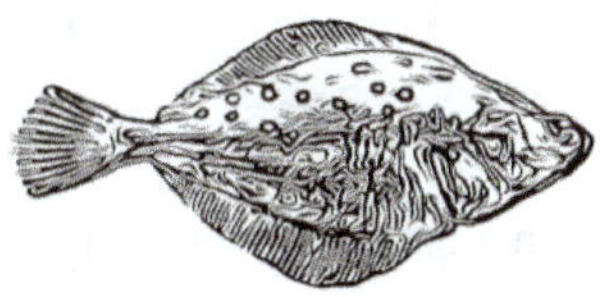

Spit explores the city as Moore goes undercover in a *Vancouver vagary voyageur montage.*

Moore opens mail in the mailroom at Boreal Extraction. Isla, a lovely young girl with a blonde bob, helps him find an office.

Spit longboards through Yale Town and down Main Street in Vancouver He skates along Kitsilano beach with the city skyline in the background.

Moore is on his laptop in their apartment researching. Spit sings a hip hop song he wrote. Moore joins in.

Isla brings a cupcake to Moore's desk. They talk for a few moments, smiling and laughing.

Spit befriends a lost scruffy terrier-type dog in the park and brings it back to the apartment. Moore shakes his head, *no*.

Moore looks through files at Boreal Extraction offices. Pulls one out of the file drawer and reads it intently.

Spit skateboards with the new dog on the front of the board.

Moore is on his laptop having breakfast. Spit comes out of his bedroom, groggy.

"Hey bud, How's work?" Spit asks, pouring a cup of coffee.

"It's OK. Have you found a job yet?"

"No."

"Have you looked?"

"Man, I consider my job as moral support and man-at-the-ready to your endeavors. Not to mention, I worked five years of my life in just two months on that fishing boat you dragged me on."

"True." Moore pauses, thinking. "As my man-at-the-ready, I need you to call this person about his work at Oro Sangriente?"

"Whore Oh, Sangria, what?"

"I found out that Oro Sangriente sold their interest in the mine just a few years back."

"OK. Didn't Vovo tells us that more than one company bailed over the years."

"She did, but what I can't understand is that they paid $181 million, the minerals are worth $500 billion with a 'b', and they gave away their shares."

"Wha'?" Spit grunts with cereal hanging out of his mouth.

"Think about it. You buy twenty pot plants because you have researched enough to know they'll be worth $10,000 by the fall. You run short of cash, and you need to sell. Do you just give them away?"

"No, man. I'd try to sell just a part."

"What if your mom is busting your chops that you need to get rid of the plants in the yard?"

"I guess I'd still try to only sell some of it. If I had to sell all for under market, I'd try to find a buyer who would let me buy them back when I was flush."

"Exactly. I don't think Oro Sangriente is out of the deal."

"Whoa, man. Don't get us killed based on your theories."

"Chicken."

Spit shrugs. He bounces his head to his music.

"I just need you to call this dude who they fired. Maybe he'll have some information. I'd call, but I'll be at work. You know, that thing that pays for our food."

"Text me his info and what you want me to ask."

"Thanks, bud."

CHAPTER 22
STARRY FLOUNDER
{PLATICHTHYS STELLATUS}

"I called a guy about the Green Amendment," Camas says, running along the shore of Lake Bijou Nez.

Tilly is with Liam at the Fisherman Bar having a beer.

"What did you find out?"

"He's a green lobbyist."

"Isn't that an oxymoron?" Tilly questions.

"I did ask him who is paying him. He said he didn't mind telling me but not over the phone."

"Huh? Sounds a bit sketch."

"Anyway, he's a major proponent of the green amendment and works with environmental activist groups in each state."

"Did you set up a meeting?"

"Yeah. He said he hasn't been in Alaska in five years and he'll come to you. I'll be there by then too."

"OK, great! I miss you."

"One more thing. I'm pretty sure he was speaking in iambic trimeter."

Moore and Spit head bang at a rave dance party in Vancouver. The DJ plays melodic EDM as Spit dances wildly. Moore has expert dance skills but shows more restraint. They shout over the music.

"Man, when I close my eyes, I can see red salmon swimming in beautiful crystal aqua blue water," Spit says, high.

"K," Moore responds, high also, watching the DJ.

"And I see some tiny kids in fishing waders catching fish."

"K," Moore dances.

"I think they're our kids, man. Well, not our kids, but kids we have with totally hot babes, like my girl Anika, and the imaginary hot girl you haven't met yet."

"I might have met her."

"Wow, man. Cool."

They don't speak for a few minutes, moving to the music side by side.

"I spoke with the Oro dude. My job for today."

Moore straightens up. He opens his eyes wider and faces Spit.

"What did he say?"

"He had a lot of pent up anger, man. A lot. Like, I asked him if he could smoke some pot to mellow out, and I'd call back, but when he said he doesn't smoke pot, I just wanted to get him into an Alaska intervention. Ya' know, make him fish with a lot of stinky dudes for two months. Kick his angry ass on nature. I..."

Moore interrupts. "Spit, what did he say?"

"When I asked him about Oro Sangriente, OS, Oh Shit for short, he said that they're not out. They did a side deal. Some type of agreement that if the mine goes through, they can buy phase two stock at a lower set price. Just like you thought, man."

"Shit. Good work."

"Did you just call me the shit."

"You are the shit. Good job, man," Moore says with a pat on the back.

"And, remember when we were at Vovo's cleaning the room, and the devil-Colonel-Sanders look-alike walked in?"

Moore is totally straight now and glued to Spit's words. "Yup."

"He said the name Ko," Spit reminds him.

"Yeah, that Ko was going to step up with some cheddar."

"Exactly. Well, the CEO of Oh Shit is some dude named Ko Breguante. I doubt a kawinkidink."

"We've got to get proof of that."

"You aim so high, brother. I love that about you."

They turn to watch the DJ, moving to the beat.

CHAPTER 23

RED IRISH LORD
{HEMILEPIDOTUS
HEMILEPIDOTUS}

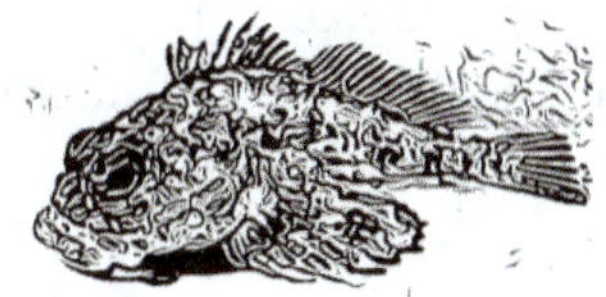

A short, heavy-set, young woman with brown hair with bangs and glasses walks out of Alaska Governor Pallie Crosfingerbak's office.

"Bea, I'll make sure to follow through on that. Safe travels."

The governor, an attractive woman in her fifties with shoulder-length auburn hair and wire-frame oval glasses, wearing a black dress with a matching black jacket, welcomes Tilly and Camas into her office. They sit across from the governor at her desk.

"Thank you for meeting with us, governor," Tilly says.

"How can I help?"

"We're trying to help with the efforts of the green amendment, so states can protect the environment within the state constitutions with a goal of it becoming an amendment to the constitution of the United States."

"Some of my constituents have asked me about that."

"What do you mean they've asked you?" Camas asks.

"They've written me a lot of letters, and called me and visited me."

"Are you pursuing it?" Tilly asks.

"I have a lot on my plate right now."

"It could help stop the Copper Cobra mine."

"Perhaps."

"Will you support it?" Tilly asks.

"I have a lot of priorities," she says, twisting her pearls, "but I will do my best."

"Thank you. We would like to request that the constitutional amendment include a "No Indian givers" clause," Tilly says.

"Excuse me?"

"You know, no mulligans, no do-overs," Camas adds.

"I don't understand."

"The protections must be irrevocable. Some general language in the green constitutional amendment about rights to clean air, water, and environment isn't enough. Time and time again, communities fight back to stop a greedy company from pillaging its natural resources only to have it rear its ugly head years later, a horrifying ghoul scratching out of the grave with long gruesome fingernails, some new configuration of shylocks from the past attempts. Like the Copper Cobra mine."

"Nice image, sista."

"Thanks."

"No Indian givers," Camas repeats, nodding her head.

"I don't know. That's not PC whatsoever."

"People think it's a derogatory phrase about Native Americans who gave gifts, but among Native Americans, it's a derogatory term about the white man who gave them promises that were never kept. Vast sacred lands given, then taken back. Promises to fish our lands forever, then big dams built. Dastardly mines defeated, then reborn."

"Still, I'm not sure now is the time to educate people on that phrase. It might offend people."

Camas stands up. Tilly knows that look in her eye and puts her hand on her arm to calm her.

"Listen up, Madame Governor." Camas's voice is strong and firm. "In case you haven't noticed, this planet's going to hell in a handbasket and not on an evening stroll but a rocket blaster. The temperature is rising so fast that, besides 100,000 salmon frying in the lethal-hot low waters last season, insurance companies are ramping up teams of disaster adjusters on standby waiting for the next hurricane or wind storm or firestorm or flood, or who knows what crazy-shit thing, to hit."

The governor raises her eyebrows and looks questioningly at Tilly. Tilly sits up proudly and listens respectfully to her best friend.

Camas becomes more passionate, raising her voice. "There have been so many unraveled environmental protections recently that the ghosts of John Muir, Rachel Carson, Edward Abbey, Doug Thompson, Wangari Maathai, Hank Thoreau, and Chico Mendes all showed up in a dream I had. JSYK, I prefer sexy dreams—well, Abbey was pretty sexy— and so things must be pretty damn bad, I thought, to see this esteemed cast of earth-heads as fluorescent green holograms at the foot of my king-size bed!"

The mayor looks very uncomfortable.

"And you know what they told me?" Camas pauses. She speaks slowly, condescendingly, but still loudly, "They told me we might not succeed!"

"Succeed at what?" The governor asks.

Camas shakes her head, then raises her hands to either side of her face and exhales loudly. Tilly takes a deep breath too.

"You are in the most important position in this state to help get this mine defeated for once and for all. And I must say your past performance has been extremely lackluster," Camas says.

The governor looks offended.

"When you say, 'it's not a priority,' we all know that's code for 'no one's paid me enough to make it one.'

The governor stands up, indignantly.

"That's good. Stand up. Get mad. Get fuckin' mad." Camas sticks her chest out further. "Why don't you take a punch? Take a punch at the earth-ghosts' messiah!"

The governor picks up the phone at her desk as if to call for help. Tilly takes Camas by the arm. "Cam, we better go."

"Thank you for seeing us, Madame Governor." Tilly leads Camas by the arm towards the door. Camas walks out.

Tilly turns around and walks back calmly to stand at the front of the governor's desk. "We might not *succeed* in surviving on the planet."

Tilly walks out the door.

"No Indian givers!!" Camas shouts from down the hall.

CHAPTER 24

PINK SALMON
{ONCHORHYNCHUS GORBUSCHA}

Tilly and Frida walk into Sacred Salmon Yoga Studio, which sits on the outskirts of Nawgek and has a wall of windows that looks out at the bay. They join nine Alaska Native women of various ages and sizes and Vovo, standing bent over, touching her toes in a stretch.

"Vovo, I want to introduce you to my dear friend, Frida," Tilly says.

"Hello, Vovo. Tilly has told me so much about you." Frida embraces Vovo.

Vovo hugs Frida and kisses her on the cheek, "Likewise. I am so thrilled to meet you."

The instructor chats with some of the students. Tilly and Frida put their mats on either side of Vovo.

"Ulaakut (*Oo-lah-coot*), good morning, ladies. Let's get started,"

Tilly turns to Vovo, "I asked Frida to come to help us."

"I have an idea for you two," Vovo says.

The class begins, and the women follow the instructor in slow, gentle yoga moves. A grizzly bear walks casually in front of the studio window, and the yogis do not flinch.

The sun sets over the water with glowing downtown Anchorage office buildings with Denali peak in the distance. Governor Crosfingerback walks along the street on her phone.

"Two young women visited me about the mine."

"So what," Dew responds impatiently.

"They had some novel ideas regarding fighting the mine."

"Pallie, what the hell does novel mean?"

"It means they scared me a little."

"We've got Bea Laurels and Prewitt Mountain on board, so why should I worry about a couple of little girls?"

Vovo leads Frida into the annual Yup'ik Native Corporation, YNC, shareholder meeting in a large warehouse space of a fish processing plant. The president of the YNC presents general business for the meeting. Tilly, Frida, and Vovo sit close to the front of the room.

"We have a guest today. Vovo..."

The Alaskan Native shareholders, especially the women, clap and call Vovo's name out. Vovo walks energetically to the front, holding Frida's hand.

"My dear friends, I have someone I would like you to meet. Her name is Frida, and she comes from the far north of Canada. I ask that you open your hearts and listen."

Most of the audience nod their head in respect. Frida walks to the microphone.

"Thank you, Vovo. It is a great privilege to speak with you. I live in Sandglass. I moved there as a child because my parents died when I was just three years old."

Murmurs of apologies are heard from the audience.

"I am from a small town about three hours outside of Yellow Knife in the Northern Territories of Canada. Not unlike here, it is always dark in the winter and always light in the summer. My people are the Tlicho. We live under the guidance of a spirit, part man, part dog."

Some shareholders nod, familiar with the tribe.

"I was just born when the mining exploration started for a uranium mine near the Marian River, where my people fished and celebrated in similar ways to you, honoring the earth and our ancestors. Our living was made off the land. The name of the mine was Rayrock, and my people would gather there several times a year, arriving by canoe or dogsled, to set up camp on the rocks or visit the families that lived in houses along the shoreline. There were annual hunts for beaver, muskrats, moose, lynx, fox, duck, geese, and fish. In those days, the animals were large and fat. The land was healthy. Berries and healing plants were plentiful. We used these lands to gather, and they brought us abundance in body and spirit."

The crowd listens intently.

"When the mine came in, they didn't tell us of the radiation. Our people do not believe in waste, and so they would use things left by the mine in a dumpsite. They never told us that these things would kill us. My parents were hired to live in the small town at the mine. The water and soil were so contaminated that plants and trees turned white with yellow cores. Our dogs had open bloody sores on their feet, our fish lost their fat and skin and had dark guts with a bad taste, beavers fur peeled off, pus was found on the meat of fish and ducks, and meat of dead carcasses turned quickly white."

Frida pauses with tears in her eyes. She closes her eyes to regain composure, then opens them. "My people got cancer and had shakes similar to those near the nuclear bombs in Japan. Fear quickly spread, and we left our beloved land altogether."

The group is silent.

"My parents died painfully from the inside out, and I was sent to live with my cousins in Sandglass. I am not here for your pity. This mine that soon will dig two miles deep into your earth, while not uranium with radiation, has as many promises of death. Nothing will contain its poison."

A woman calls out from the crowd. "They've already soiled our sacred lands with their poisoned promises. Some have followed. What can we do?"

"Those of you who are confused, seek time with your loved ones in nature. Use animals as your guides for how to fight this mine."

A small group of elders begins a low chanting.

"Know that the world is watching, your ancestors are watching, your great great great grandchildren too, and you will never *ever* regret choosing a simple life of salmon over the financial rewards of a job hauling poisons from the earth." Frida bows her head and lifts it. "Thank you, all. I wish you peace and strength."

The room erupts into applause and conversations. Many of the people come up to speak to Frida and pay their respects to Vovo.

CHAPTER 25

BARRACUDINAS
{PARALEPIDIDAE}

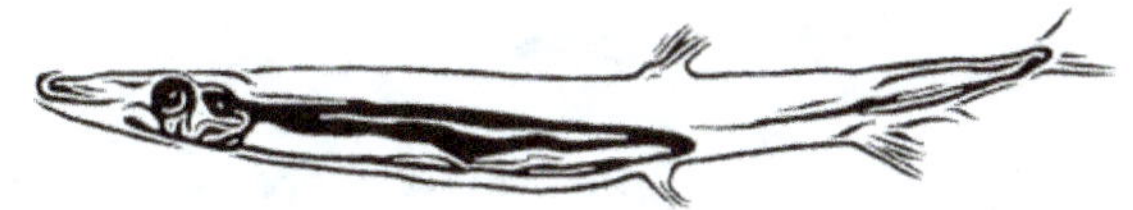

The cold and dry Alaskan winter tundra waits patiently for sockeye salmon far out in the ocean to grow and mature from a nutritious diet of small fish, crustaceans, octopus, squid, and worms.

A cabin rests in the middle of the desolate snow-covered tundra with a fire in the fireplace and smoke coming out of the chimney. Long dried, smoked salmon strips tied in round bunches fill a rustic shed on anti-bear stilts.

A large grizzly enters a hut-like den covered in grasses. The snow falls and covers it completely, leaving no trace from above.

Far out in the ocean at night, beluga whales swim under an aurora borealis sky.

Amak and his eight-year-old son fish for smelt through a small circular cut-out in the thick ice in the middle of a lake.

A warm glow emanates from Vovo's lodge window. A tall Christmas tree decorated with simple natural ornaments and red bows stands in the corner as she talks on the phone, laughing. Black reads in his recliner.

Thomas, wearing a turn of the century long-tail waistcoat, a vest, and an ascot-style, loose, bowtie with his hair slicked back neatly, stands on a small stage in Van's Dive Bar in Anchorage. Most people pay little attention as they socialize. He pushes a button on a boom box, and a Grateful Dead song plays as he reads an excerpt from Ralph Waldo Emerson's Nature.

"The stars awaken a certain reverence because though always present, they are inaccessible, but all natural objects make a kindred impression when the mind is open to their influence."

Eve stands in front of Bart's desk in his office. "I overheard someone saying that the mine bought you."

"You know that I met with Dick Huntington," Bart responds.

"Nature never wears a mean appearance. Neither does the wisest man extort her secret and lose his curiosity by finding out all her perfection. Nature never became a toy to a wise spirit," Thomas recites through the smoky, dark bar.

"Yes, you told me that." Eve waits for him to say more.
Silence.
"They're going to pay us the same amount as their lobbyist, ten million dollars, if twenty-five percent of fishermen come to Rakoff."

"The flowers, the animals, the mountains, reflected the wisdom of his best hour, as much as they had delighted the simplicity of his childhood. When we speak of nature in this manner, we have a distinct but most poetical sense in the mind. We mean the integrity of impression made by manifold natural objects."

"Why?" Eve asks. Her face looks pained.
"I think they figure they're all sheep, and if twenty-five percent come over, the others will follow."

"It is this which distinguishes the stick of timber of the wood-cutter, from the tree of the poet. The charming land-scape, which I saw this morning, is indubitably made up of some twenty or thirty farms. Miller owns this field, Locke that, and Manning the woodland beyond. But none of them owns the landscape. There is a property in the horizon which no man has but he whose eye can integrate all the parts, that is, the poet."

"You know that the opposite is true," Eve retorts. "I've always gone along with your business wishes, even if I might have done things differently. I'm not sure I can stand by you when our lifetime of livelihood from salmon is now becoming a livelihood to kill them!"

She turns around and slams the door on her way out.

Bart looks down at his wedding band and a wedding photo on his desk.

Two people clap when Thomas finishes his spoken word performance. He turns off the boom box and steps down from the stage.

"Thanks for coming all the way to Nawgek," Tilly says, sitting with Thomas and Camas at a picnic table outside a food truck.

"I wanted to see it. You know, we could use some public awareness for the green amendment lobbying efforts."

"Camas has that dialed in. She has two million followers of her Sexy Salmon with Camas show, and her Aunt Camas Sockeye kids show has 900,000."

"Great! Hey, let's call my friend Reina at the EPA."

Thomas picks up his phone.

"Hi, Reina. What's up with the Cobra permit? Ducks in a row to nix it?"

Thomas's face drops. "No shit. That's a hit. I'm sorry, doll. See you back at the Mall."

He turns to the girls. "It's not looking good."

"Can we get the amendment before June?" Tilly asks.

"If the votes tip over, the green 'mendment line, we'll take it to congress, in the nick of time."

Tilly and Camas look at each other with raised eyebrows.

CHAPTER 26

LANTERNFISH {MYCTOPHIDAE}

"How's Vancouver? Did you meet a girl?" Vovo asks, walking along the river on her phone.

"It's fine, Vovo. Yes, I did. Her name's Isla."

"Beautiful. I met my late husband at twenty-one. He was so very handsome and took me to Anchorage to the theater. He was nervous and had sweaty palms when he held my hand, but I decided to go on a second date, anyway."

Moore laughs, "You must miss him and, Vovo, we miss you. We're calling because we need your help."

"Give me the deets."

Within a period of just a few days, Nawgek goes from a sleepy town of a few hundred people to thousands as the fishermen and fish processing workers arrive for the season.

A grizzly rummages through a small town trash can. He finds a drunk guy in a car asleep with a pizza, pulls him out, and takes the pie. "The bears are hungry. They want the salmon to get here too," a local tells an Anchorage newspaper reporter.

An airplane from Anchorage is full of men and a couple of women in knit caps with duffel bags stuffed into overhead compartments heading to Nawgek from all parts of the country.

A friendly older woman with deep creases in her face and her crew of three women sew and repair fishing nets. The fishermen come in and out all day, picking them up and dropping them off. There is a small folk band playing in the back and a few men listening and drinking beer.

Fishermen work on boat engines and systems in dry boatyards. Torden and his crew work on his boat with loud rock music playing.

Boatyards are filled with stacks of boat parts and supplies. They are beautiful in their simplicity and repetition -- anchors, engines, buoys, hanging racks of orange overalls.

The Nawgek grocery bustles with fishermen scrambling to buy food and supplies.

Jake eyes a bare shelf. "Damn, I just needed mayonnaise."

"Don't you have any eggs?" a fisherman calls out.

"I'm sorry, we're sold out."

Karima carries a large carton of eggs out the door.

"Hey, leave some for us!"

"I'm sorry. I preordered these two months ago," Karima answers. She stops, pulls a dozen eggs out, and hands them to the man.

Five large fishing boats on stands are the backdrop for exuberant corn hole games amidst a pre-fishing barbeque celebration.

"I heard Torden and Genovese took Rakoff's offer," Sloane says, watching the game with Jake, Heinz, Rod, and three other fishermen.

"It's hard to refuse," Heinz says.

"Did you consider it?" she asks pointedly.

"I was tempted. I like a sure bet. But when he offered stock in the mine to sweeten the deal, the stench poured out like a politician wearing a whore's imitation French perfume, and I snapped out of it."

"Good man," Jake says.

"I don't know how many have gone over, but we'll find out soon enough."

"Chalky called to tell me his Japanese idea didn't pan out," Sloane says to Heinz.

"I questioned his Robin Hood cred," Heinz replies.

"It was worth a shot," Sloane responds.

"Amak told me they've surveyed the site and are having a

fancy ribbon-cutting party to break ground on June 17th, "
Rod says.

"On fucking fishing opening day," Heinz says.

"Of course it is," Jake says solemnly.

"Here's your ticket to King Salmon," Prewitt says, handing
Reina a piece of paper in the company cafeteria line.

"Why would I be going there?"

"We're presenting the permit at a gala. The president
wants the EPA to show solidarity with the Army Corps of
Engineers when Boreal Extraction breaks ground at the
dinner."

"Great," Reina says, exasperated. "Not only am I going to
have nightmares about working here when that monstrosity
was approved, but I'm also going to hear the screaming earth
in my sleep."

"Grow some balls, McCaring," he says as he walks away.

Reina throws a veggie burger onto her plate angrily as she
talks out loud to herself. "How can a single human being take
a quarter of a million dollars from fossil fuel..." She stabs at
the salad bar. "... try to stamp out affordable health care,
women's reproductive rights, and gay rights..." her voices
raises, "*and* be on team Copper Cobra?!"

Another employee looks at her curiously.

Reina violently scoops some fries onto her plate and
throws the tongs down. "I've got balls, asshole," she says
under her breath.

Eve and Bart are asleep in their king-size bed. Bart tosses and turns then becomes agitated. He grimaces and has a look of terror on his face.

A vivid nightmare with images of heaps upon heaps of dead, bloated salmon filling the river and its banks and the shoreline of the bay fill his mind. He hears loud crackly buzzing, like sizzling cheese on a casserole, the mounds of maggots eating the fish flesh.

"Aaaaaaaaugh!!" Bart screams, rising.

"What is it? What is it, dear?!"

Bart holds his head in his hands. "It's nothing," he says weakly. "Just a bad dream."

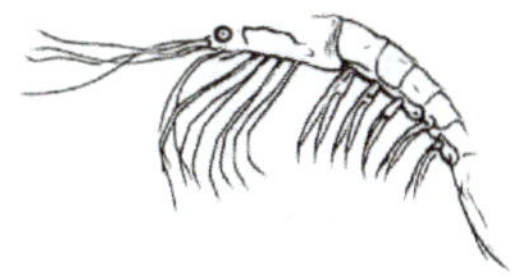

The reflection of the city skyline can be seen in the exterior windows of the Vancouver Aquarium with its undulating dramatic roofline. Inside, Moore and Spit sit on either side of Vovo, looking at a graceful beluga whale swimming behind floor to ceiling glass.

"What's the mission, gentlemen?"

"You have an appointment with Dick Huntington regarding the land you own adjacent to the mine site. He thinks you're interested in selling it," Moore says.

"How did you get that appointment, clever boys?"

"I met his assistant. She's the girl I mentioned. Isla. I think she likes me."

"As well she should. Go on."

"Spit is going to be your driver. At your age..."

Moore stops, not wanting to offend their dear Vovo.

"You can say it. 'At my age.' I'm 106, for Christ's sake."

She grabs their hands for a quick squeeze, and Moore and Spit smile.

"At your age, they won't question that you need to have

Spit with you. We just need you to be with The Dick long enough for Spit to find a file on their computer."

"I'll bring you to the meeting. You need to act your actual age, not the forty-esque you are," Spit says.

"You boys are so charming," she smiles.

"When you're meeting with Dick, Spit will go to the restroom and find a computer to get the file. I'd get it myself, but I'm more of the creative type, not the hacker-whiz like Spit."

"Thanks, man," Spit says proudly.

"When's the appointment?" Vovo asks.

"Tomorrow at 9:30 am."

"Let's synchronize our watches," Vovo says, pulling her cuff back to expose her watch.

The boys pull out their phones. The sweet-faced beluga is looking at the three of them.

"That whale is trying to tell us something," Spit says.

"They live in arctic regions, including Bristle Bay. He's asking us to save his family and the tasty salmon he likes to eat from the poison waters of the mine," Moore says.

"And to break him out of here," Spit adds.

"Smart boys."

CHAPTER 28
SCALE WORM {POLYNOIDAE}

The town is abuzz as a few salmon begin to arrive, and there are reports that the mass of salmon will arrive in just a few days. Jake rushes into the fishing supply store to pick up a repaired part for his engine. The store clerk is a friendly young man in Nawgek for his first season.

"How's it going?" Jake says a bit gruffly. "Jake Selkirk. I'm here to pick up a part."

"Let me go check on that," the clerk says as he hurries to the back.

Amak walks in. "Hi, Jake," he says with a warm smile.

"How are the counts?"

"Looks like we're going to have our minimums early, and you all should be off to the races."

"Where are they? I listened to the radio yesterday, but not yet today."

"I don't think it's as easy to predict anymore due to the climate. Last year the fish had to stop and wait when the temperatures were too high. You know we lost 100,000 in the heat. Their movement is sporadic again this year too."

"They're on the way, and we're grateful. There's a lot of tundra cotton this year. That's always a good omen."

"Are you going to the Cobra meeting Thursday?"

"Yes."

"I'm in complete shock this thing is happening," Amak says, grabbing something from the shelf.

"It's not happening."

"Are you in denial?"

"I'm a realist. But I'm also a captain. I may not run the top crews anymore as I did for twenty-five years, but I'll stop those money-whoring bastards if it kills me."

Jake walks out, his strong towering frame showing wear from his years fishing and the torment of the mine.

"Don't let it!" Amak calls out.

Amak stands in front of a class of twelve kindergarten students. They sit on the floor in a semi-circle, and he sits on a kid's chair. The children are Alaska Natives, including a boy named Sax, except for one girl with blonde hair named Willow.

"Where do salmon live?" Amak asks with playful reverence.

"In the water," a girl answers.

"That's right. What kind of water?"

"The lakes?"

"Yes, where else?"

The children look around at each other and their teacher.

"The river," Willow answers.

"Yes, good."

"One more place. Who knows where else the salmon live?"

"The sky?" an Alaska Native girl says.

"Hmmm. Why do you say that?"

"My mom says that the northern lights are animal spirits, including the salmon."

The kids look at each other, nodding.

"Very good. Well then, I guess there were two more places. The sky and?"

The kids shrug their shoulders.

Amak answers. "The ocean."

The children nod, "Oh, yeah."

"I knew that," Sax says confidently.

"Very good. Sockeye got their name when people tried to translate a Native language from 'suk-key,' meaning red fish. The sockeye are born in a lake where they live for one to three years. Then they travel to the sea where they get big and strong. They stay there one to four years, and then here comes the magic..."

"Magic!?" the children say with wide eyes.

"The salmon make their way all the way back up the river to the lake where they were born, sometimes within just a few feet, where they lay eggs to make baby salmon. After they lay their eggs, both the females and males die."

"That's sad," Willow says.

The teacher, an Alaska Native woman in her late twenties, adds, "It is a little sad that the babies don't get to meet their parents."

"It's also a miracle that their parents make it back at all. Only about four in 1,000 come back because they have many challenges in the sea and their travels. They feed other animals, like whales in the ocean, and grizzly bears in the river."

The children's eyes get wide when they hear the word grizzly.

"And we fish for them," Sax says.

"That's right."

"What if we catch all of them?"

"That's an excellent question. You're allowed to fish to eat during the year, but the fishermen with nets are controlled by people like me, and they can only fish when a certain number of salmon have passed through. We tell them "go" and "stop," and if they don't listen, they have to pay a big fine."

"What's a fine?"

"It's money," says Willow. "My dad had to pay that once. He was really mad."

"Yes, they do get mad, but better mad at us than no more salmon, right?"

"Right!" The kids yell.

"Do you know an easy way to remember the five types of salmon?"

"With our five fingers, Amak?" The young teacher asks, playing along.

"That's right! Hold out your thumb," Amak instructs.

The children all hold their thumbs up.

"Chum rhymes with thumb. Chum is also a smaller fish, like our thumbs. Can you say chum?"

"Chum!" The children shout.

"Great! Your middle finger..."

The kids start to raise their fingers.

"No, no kids, just hold up your entire hand," the teacher says, demonstrating.

Amak laughs, "Your biggest finger is the king. The king is the big honcho of the kingdom, so just remember middle finger, king. Rings are silver, so your ring finger is the silver salmon, also called coho. And our pinky finger helps us remember Pink salmon. Their flesh is light-colored, and some people call them 'humpies' because of a hump they get when they spawn. OK, we saved the best for last. What finger do we have left?"

The children hold up their pointer fingers.

"You could poke someone's eye with your finger — don't do it! So our pointer is for the sockeye."

Amak and the teacher raise their red index fingers, and the children excitedly follow.

CHAPTER 29

SPOTTED SEAL {PHOCA LARGHA}

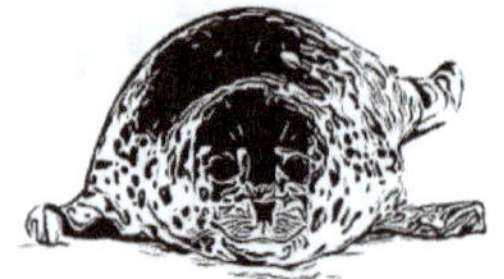

R*aise it red!* goes viral from Camas on camera in her diligent daily smart, spunky, and sexy anti Copper Cobra videos.

A little girl colors her pointer finger red with her colored marker in a kindergarten class. The teacher looks confused. The other kids copy her.

A heavyset, bearded Hells Angels biker in a denim vest with many tattoos sits in a tattoo chair with an even tougher looking tattoo artist. He holds up his newly tattooed red pointer finger delicately.

A sophisticated businesswoman stands in front of a conference table, making a presentation. She points to a chart with her red pointer finger.

The New York Giants and the Dallas Cowboys stand as a celebrity sings the national anthem, their hands on their heart with a dyed-red index finger. When the song ends, they put their red fingers in the air and run onto the field.

The kindergarten class that Amak visited raise their hands in class. All of their pointer fingers are red.

Talk show host Jimmy Fallon interviews Camas dressed in a full-size salmon suit with the front open to expose her cleavage. At the end, they both hold up a dyed-red pointer finger.

CHAPTER 30
SEA PORK {APLIDIUM CALIFORNICUM}

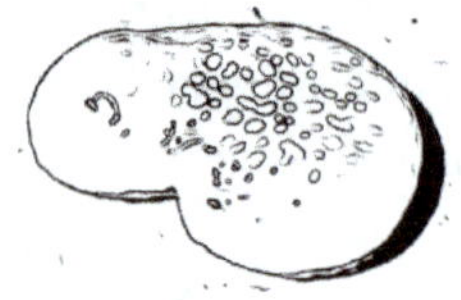

Moore drops Vovo and Spit off around the corner from the Boreal Extraction entrance.

"I'll be going around the block until you text me. Head south on Albino Street, and I'll find you. Good luck."

Vovo walks energetically at her regular pace from the car to the corner near the office entrance, then suddenly acts like a decrepit old lady as she walks the rest of the distance and into the building, Spit holding her arm.

"Vovo Selkirk for Dick Hunterson," Spit says to the receptionist. He has his hand over Vovo's on his arm. She leans forward in pretend osteoporosis.

"Have a seat, please."

Vovo plays it up. "Oh, I'm too old to sit. My bones don't bend anymore. I'm a hundred and six."

"There's a wall over there if you need to lean," the receptionist offers.

"Leaning will be good."

Vovo and Spit walk over to the wall, and he pretends to

lean her against it. Still within earshot of the receptionist, Vovo says, "Just lean me up like a green popsicle stick, icy and stiff."

Spit laughs. Under his breath, "I like popsicles."

"Hello, Mrs. Selkirk," Dick says as he walks up to shake her hand. "Who's this?"

"This is Jiles. He's my driver. You know, hard to get around these days, and hard to find good help for that matter."

"He can stay here. I'll help you to the conference room."

Spit feigns concern, "Will you be OK, Mrs. Selkirk?"

"Yes. I won't be long."

She walks off on Dick's arm.

Spit looks around. He texts Moore: *v is in meeting. we're on!*

Spit walks down a corridor with cubicles on either side.

"Can I help you?" A man in a suit asks.

"Where's the head, man."

"The what?"

"The john... the loo. I'm a man of the sea. I don't speak Dudley Do-Right."

With a skeptical look, the man says, "It's back over there."

"Thanks."

Spit quickly turns around and heads in that direction. He sees an open computer in the corner. He ducks in and sits down, putting the computer headphones on.

He texts Moore, *shit, someone's on my case*

I told you you need a haircut!

got a computer

Get her done, bro

Spit types quickly and looks around over his shoulder. Two young female employees notice him and stop at the cubicle.

"Hi there," the girls say flirtatiously with smiles.

"Damn viruses. Got to get this machine cleaned up. I almost have it. I better get back to work," Spit says, putting his head down into the keyboard.

The girls continue walking, giggling.

Spit browses for the files and pulls up a list. He searches some words, then texts Moore: *searched oro sangriente and ko briguante nothing*

Try Yu'pik Community Partners

Spit quickly types the search.

nope

Try Yupik

Spit types.

bingo multiple files with oro, one says first right of refusal oro sangriente copper cobra mine phase ii

Get them all and get outta there! I'm at Albino and Thurston.

Spit types frantically, downloading the files. He hears Vovo's voice in an uncharacteristically loud old lady voice.

"Thank you for meeting with me, Dick."

Spit finishes the download. He ducks down onto the floor, just as Dick and Vovo pass the cubicle. He peeks out, and when Dick is out of sight, crawls out and past the opening of the next cubicle which belongs to Isla. She pulls him quickly in and hides him until the coast is clear.

"Where's your driver?" Dick asks.

"He's probably out taking a toke," Vovo says in her youthful voice, standing straighter. She catches herself. "Probably taking a leak," she says in an old lady voice.

Isla walks into the reception area with Spit. "Here he is. He looked lost, so I helped him."

"Jiles, take me home," Vovo says.

Spit holds out his arm, and Vovo holds onto it as he leads her slowly to the elevator. Vovo winks at Isla just before the elevator door closes. Dick looks over at Isla with a stern look.

Vovo and Spit run out of the elevator and office lobby onto the street, then down the block to hop into the getaway Scout with Moore.

CHAPTER 31

BERING WOLFFISH {ANARHICHAS ORIENTALIS}

An immense barge enters the Seattle commercial fishing port with a piece of machinery the size of an ocean liner on top. The dark, ominous bucket-wheel excavator is as tall as a 30-story building and has a 70-foot bucket-wheel. The reflection off of its twenty steel-bladed buckets is blinding. Dew and Dick stand on the dock as six tugboats maneuver the barge.

"You went all the way there, didn't you?" Dew says.

"I told you you didn't need to come down here," Dick responds, annoyed.

"The hell I didn't. I'm surprised the picketers aren't here already. I wanted to monitor the opposition." He stares straight up at the goliath beast. "That's unnamable."

"It's a Bagger 300. 15,000 tons and can move 13,000,000 cubic feet of earth a day. Takes five guys to run, but it's a slashing monster."

"Christ, why so goddamn big, Dick? We can't hide that."

"We need to get that copper outta there. Once the reality hits the dumb folks convinced their future wealth is built on this mine, we'll be all alone."

"You mean all the dead fish?"

"Our only hope is that the climate gets the fish first."

"You might be in luck there."

"In and out. Get the earth screaming for its life before the people do."

"In and out probably means you won't owe Oro a penny either."

One of Dick's gold fillings sparkles as it reflects off the Bagger blades as he opens his mouth slightly in a sinister smile.

"What in the world are you doing?" Moore asks Spit.

"I'm practicing my dancing," Spit says, ballroom dancing with a fishing pole in front of Vovo's lodge.

"Since when do you ballroom dance?"

"Since Anika told me I had to learn."

"She's got you hooked," Moore says, making a fishing motion with his arm.

Spit smiles and keeps dancing. Moore answers his phone.

"I told Chalky about the papers you got," Sloane says, from the wheel of her boat, drydocked in the boatyard.

"Yeah. What'd he say?" Moore says anxiously.

"Looks like it might not be admissible in court, considering the way you got it."

"Shit. What if instead of from Spit, it came from a former employee?"

"I'll find out. Stand by. Over."

"Roger. Over."

"I need you to call the Oro guy and see if he's mad enough to say that he had those papers already."

"Hey man, that's fibbing."

"It's not like we fabricated the document." Moore puts on a sad, dramatic face. "And the fishies, man."

Spit shrugs.

"OK, OK, no perjury. Damn your morals, Fred Astaire."

Spit lays the rod down in a dancing dip. "We'll find another way, bud."

CHAPTER 32
SMOOTH LUMPSUCKER
{APTOCYCLUS VENTRICOSUS}

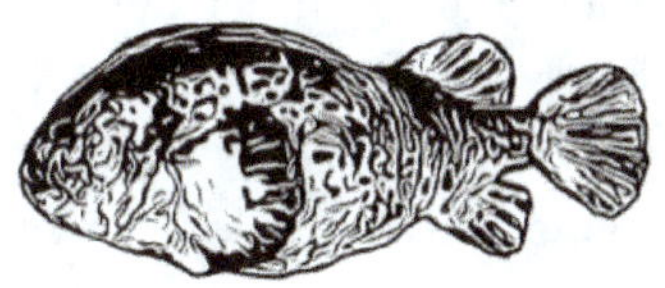

Ko sits at his desk with a teacup chihuahua lying on top of a newspaper on the desk. He notices an article on the Copper Cobra mine inside. He pulls the paper out from under the dog quickly. The dog nearly falls off the desk and growls at Ko.

"Hunterson has brought in the Bagger. That son of a bitch is trying to get in and out before Phase II."

Aila Abzug, a green activist known for taking risks to protect the environment, joins Chalky at a fancy San Francisco white tablecloth restaurant with a view of the Golden Gate Bridge. Aila is 5'2" with dark, shoulder-length hair and wears a tight-fitting low-cut wrap-dress.

"Aila, how's your mother?"

"As feisty as ever," Aila says with a slight New Jersey accent. She pulls out a long vape cigarette holder reminiscent of a 1930s film noir movie star.

"She must be proud of your accomplishments."

"They never live up to her dam busting days, but yeah, she's happy I'm not living a traditional existence."

The waiter approaches. "I'm sorry, miss. There's no vaping in here."

"It's not vape. Nicotine sucks. It's pot."

"Pot either."

Aila puts the device back in her purse. "Oy vey. Tell me. You're a lawyer. Pot is legal in California. Why can't I smoke it in public?"

"It's quite a long answer. Aila, I asked you to lunch because there are some good people who need help to stop the Copper Cobra mine. I have an idea, and it involves you."

"I'm listening."

"I need you to buy an option for Phase II of the mine from Oro Sangriente."

"The Sienna Green Club has been good to me, but I don't have money to buy a mine."

"I just need you to be the negotiator between a foreign buyer and Oro and convince them to sell their option."

"I still don't understand."

"I'll do all the leg-work. Get the company lined up," he winks twice dramatically, "prepare the documents, and you just need to get them to agree to sell in the form of a letter of intent."

Aila is silent.

"What are you thinking?"

"You're asking me to get them to sell something I don't even understand?"

"Yes."

"I can sell anything, so I'm not worried about that. What are the stakes?"

"50 million wild salmon per year multiplied by infinity. And your mother will be proud."

Aila looks out over the Bay.

"I'll do it."

"Ko Breguante's a scoundrel, so use your wiles."

"I've got those," she says, glancing down at her cleavage.

CHAPTER 33
PACIFIC SANDFISH {TRICHODON TRICHODON}

Jake stands in front of a large room in a fish processing plant with 1,500 fishermen. Black, Vovo, Moore, and Spit are in the front row. Heinz and Sloane are one row back.

"You've all heard the Alaskan proverb 'you never really know your friends from your enemies until the ice breaks,'" Jake says passionately. "The mine has completely infiltrated every aspect of our livelihoods. Rakoff is buying you shares of the mine. The mine bribes locals with stock. Mining partners are giving Native organizations shares and buying entire communities off with large payoffs in the name of education and future jobs. We still have a majority here who say they're anti-mine, but many of those are being swayed every day."

The crowd nods.

"The only way I believe we can show the community, these mining bastards, and the world, our solidarity, to have any chance at all..."

Bart and Eve Rakoff walk into the back of the room. Jake pauses.

He continues even more loudly, "... is not to fish this season!"

The crowd gasps. There is pandemonium as many of the fishermen erupt in an emotional uproar.

"Are you joking?! That's the most asinine idea you've ever had, big Jake!" an older fisherman shouts from the crowd.

"I need this money. I have loans on my boat, and my house back home," another shouts.

"You know that for most of us, this is our entire income for the year."

"And for our crews and the processors!" A female voice shouts.

"My entire family works the season!" Fisherman Lou says.

"You're wealthy, you don't..."

"No!" Jake says in a strong booming voice, holding up his hand. The crowd quiets.

"No, I am not wealthy! I came here with a few hundred dollars and rented the deadliest fall-apart boat I could afford. That boat almost killed me, but I slowly built my way to a living, not unlike many of you."

"Let's vote!" Sloane calls out.

"If a majority agrees, I don't have to follow," Torden shouts from the back of the crowd.

"No one has to do anything here," Jake responds strongly. "However, that seems to have gotten us into a lot of trouble so far. Does anyone have anything else to say before we vote?"

There is silence.

"OK, then..."

Moore clears his throat loudly and stands up very straight. "Captain, I'd like to say something."

Jake is surprised. He sees Vovo's stern face nod at him, and he tries to hide his skepticism. "Yes, Moore," he says with a nod. Then loudly, unsmiling, "This is my crewman, Moore DeMontagne."

The restless crowd watches Moore walk to the front while they chatter and grumble.

Jake turns to him, "Young man, now is not time to hold back." Jake takes a seat next to Vovo, and she puts her hand over his.

Moore clears his throat again. "Fishing for salmon is not unlike mining," he shouts over the noisy group.

Jake, shocked, stands back up. The crowd is suddenly silent. "What?!" and "Did you hear...?" fill the thick air. Vovo pulls Jake back down into his seat.

Moore looks Jake in the eye. "You're taking something from nature, salmon, to sell for profit. Just like mining."

The fishermen continue rough chatter and a bit of heckling.

"What about those Aces?" Spit says to the person sitting next to him, feeling the tension in the crowd. Then he looks up to Moore and makes eye contact, "You go, buddy!"

The crowd does not quiet. Muffled rumbling and words of discontent fill the room.

Vovo stands with her back to the crowd. The crowd quiets.

"You are absolutely right, Moore. Good for you." Vovo turns to speak to the crowd of fishermen behind her. "Our fishing and tribal legacies are to listen before deciding. Continue please, Moore." She says regally, then with a firm, loud spanking voice, "Johnny and Spark, if you don't shut the hell up, I'm calling your mothers."

You could hear a pin drop.

"In the fifties, after motors arrived, we fished and fished and then overfished until there were no more fish. It took changes and regulations to count fish and limit our boat size to thirty-two feet. Sure, there's still dishonesty, people not following the rules...," he looks across the room to Torden. Moore continues strongly, "but, you, or the fishermen before you, and the Native people of this land, knew that if we didn't protect this place, we would have nothing left."

The crowd listens quietly.

"It was painful to have to scale back, to set limits, but you did." He pauses. "... and the salmon came back."

Some people in the group nod their heads. There is a low hum of voices.

Moore speaks louder, "If we can make the same... OK, not the same. If we can make an even bigger sacrifice, maybe we can save the salmon again. But this time,"

He speaks louder, "forever."

Quiet again in the crowd.

"What is honor? The dictionary says it is adherence to what is *right* or to a conventional standard of conduct. And what is *right?*"

He pauses, looking out into the crowd.

"Maybe the mine has seeped in because somewhere over these years of fishing in greed and gluttony, at the expense of the people who have lived here for generations, the mine slipped in like a wolf in the wolf house."

Some gasps. The majority listen intently.

"Under sail, perhaps due to the dangers of the sea, the fishermen helped each other. When motors came, so did bankers and lawyer fishermen. A tough lot, but a tough lot with the money to buy a big shove-you-around boat. When the small print rules came that city folk could easily figure out, who here gave his permit back to the fifty-year-old Native elder who had fished this bay for forty-three years?"

Murmuring rises from the crowd as the brave words incite.

"Maybe if we want the mine to have honor, we need to have honor ourselves and create gentlemen's rules." Moore looks at Sloane "and ladies'. Not to be weak, but to save the salmon and the sacredness of what we do. We are different from the mine. This, I truly believe. We are different, proud brothers and sisters of Bristle Bay, because..."

Moore holds up his red pointer finger.

The crowd is glued to the words.

"... we do not need to *take* everything to *have* everything."

There is a roar of voices and applause in the crowd as many fishermen jump to their feet. Vovo grabs Jake and Spit's hands and rises. Moore walks off the stage. Vovo and Spit hug him and Spit plants an exuberant kiss on his cheek.

"Let's vote!" Black shouts over the loud crowd. "Use the weigh tags being distributed!"

CHAPTER 34

DECORATED WARBONNET
{CHIROLOPHIS SNYDERI}

Camas is diligent in her daily Sexy Salmon with Camas videos. "2011. 145,454 gallons of copper tailings. Equipment malfunction," Camas reads in her sexy evening gown, her Marilyn Monroe voice expressing dismay over the horrific mine spills. "2006. 660,000 gallons of arsenic water. Cracked pipe."

The Bagger 300 is put back together at the Copper Cobra mine site after traveling from the port. Large cranes lift various pieces and put them into place like a gargantuan sci-fi lego set. Loud noises from the machinery cause animals to scatter. A crane lifts the large 20-bucket wheel onto the machine.

"1998. Acid rock drainage. Clogged pipe. 1990. Dust emissions pollute the air. 2011. 290,000 gallons of copper acid tailings. Cause unknown. 2007. 1.2 million gallons of arsenic water. Cold temperatures. 2006. 270,000 gallons of acid water. Pump failure. 2006. 1,000,000 gallons of mine process water. Failed indicator. 2000. 110 tons of ore slurry. Leak in ore line. 2000. 18,000 tons of sulfuric acid. Flange failure."

Ceremonies, small and large, express gratitude for the arrival of the first salmon with prayers to defeat the mine.

A multi-generation fishing family prepares their small fishing dwelling on the shore. They catch the first salmon of the season and place it reverently in the middle of a wood table. An elder woman slices it into pieces, and each person takes a bite. They bow their heads in thanks for the first salmon.

Six Alaska Native children ages seven through twelve run and play, laughing, near lake Iliana with small backpacks. They come upon four Boreal Extraction trucks. A boy opens up his pack, and it is full of black raven feathers.

Small, medium, and large groups of people, indigenous and others, gather in opposition to the mine. Many have their index fingers painted red and sit in sacred meditation and prayer.

CHAPTER 35
GIANT BARNACLE {BALANUS EVERMANNI}

Black and Fisherman Lou count the ballots. Many fishermen pace and walk around outside.

"We've got the vote!"

Jake stands at the podium. Lou walks to the front and hands Jake the results.

In a booming voice, Jake reads, "Out of 1,513 boats, 1,335 voted to not fish and head to the mine." His voice lowers. "178 boats voted to fish."

Jake bows his head, deflated. He is unable to speak, and the mic drops to the floor. Torden puffs out his chest at the news.

Black picks up the mic and turns to Jake, "Thank you, son. Thank all of you for your passion and hard work." He speaks to the crowd, "There is no one wrong here. I know every single one of you cares for this community and the salmon." Slowly, carefully, in sadness, he says, "I guess we will just adjourn."

"Wait!" A woman calls out from the back of the room. The crowd turns around. Eve grabs Bart's hand and runs, dragging him towards the front of the room.

There are soft murmurs, "Oh, Eve," and heartfelt looks of affection for her as they arrive at the front and face the crowd.

"Eve, what are we doing up here? Do you have something to say?" Bart asks.

"Hello, my dear friends. Yes, *we* have something to say about this critical matter. Stand by. Over."

The crowd is quiet with respect for beautiful Eve. Eve turns her back to the group and quietly and says to the man that she loves deeply, "Repeat after me if you still wish to be married."

Bart looks startled and mouths, "Alright."

Eve reaches up on her tiptoes, cups her hand to his ear, and whispers. Bart listens. He raises his eyebrows to her. She nods a go-ahead motion.

"We will pay you for this season if you don't fish and instead go to the mine," Bart says tentatively.

Bart is a deer in the headlights and becomes silent. Eve turns back around and smiles sweetly at the crowd. Vovo blows her a kiss, and Eve holds her hands up in prayer to her heart, then her head. Eve begins a soft and beautiful chant. Vovo picks up the melody and puts her hands in prayer to her heart as well. Some in the crowd chant along.

Bart comes out of his trance and shouts at the top of his lungs, "I'll pay you for the season if all of you don't fish!"

The crowd erupts in applause.

"We'll match last year's payouts!" he adds.

The fishermen clap and shout. Eve throws her arms around Bart and kisses him. As she is embracing him, she gently takes the microphone and gives him a sweet smile. He smiles back.

"Plus, 20 percent!" Eve calls out to the crowd.

Bart laughs and picks her up in a hug.

Jake speaks loudly into the microphone. "Gather your crews. We'll head to the mine tonight!"

CHAPTER 36
ALEUTIAN ALLIGATORFISH
{ASPIDOPHOROIDES BARTONI}

"I'm sorry, Tilly. This may sound silly. Our congress appearance was extended. Delaying the timing planet will be mended," Thomas rhymes from the United States Capitol.

"Days?"

"No, weeks."

Tilly is deeply disappointed. "Oh, no. That's terrible! Thanks for letting me know, Thomas, and for all your hard work."

She taps her phone to call Moore.

"The green amendment won't be passed in time."

"Damn," Moore responds.

"I said I would help you, and I've failed," Tilly says, tears streaming down her face. I can't bear to think of this world without those beautiful salmon."

"It's not over yet. Here's what I need you to do!"

"I'm listening."

"Get the press rounded up because 1,500 fishing boats are abandoning fishing to protest at the mine."

"What?!"

"There's not a moment to lose."

"I'll get Camas on that straight away! She's the PR queen."

"There's one more thing. Sloane is going to call you. Spit and I found something that might still stop this goddamn thing."

"I'll be standing by. Be safe, brother."

Tilly and Sloane climb into a puddle jumper airplane at Nawgek Airport.

CHAPTER 37
COHO SALMON
{ONCHORHYNCHUS KISUTCH}

Hundreds of fishing boats embark from Nawgek and other parts of Bristle Bay and travel to the mouth of the Kojack River. The beautiful warm colors of the low sun blend with the orange of the fishing bibs and the sparkling water. The fishermen's expressions are a mix of severe and joyful as they experience the camaraderie of the singular mission to the mine, their bright red index fingers raised in the air to their fishing brothers and sisters.

Hundreds of thousands of salmon flow through Bristle Bay as Torden's high powered fishing boat travels at top speed across the water toward Eaglegek.

"Christ, we'll be rich! They're as thick as sardines," Lando exclaims, like a gold miner finding a strike.

The rest of the crew are solemn as they hydroplane over the water.

"Careful! They're too thick; you won't land clear," Six says, worried they will kill fish in the engine.

"We're OK," Torden shouts back. "I'll find a clear spot."

The boat turns quickly, and Torden stops the engine.

"Good landing, captain!" Six shouts.

"Let her go! It's the mother lode of our lives!" Torden commands.

Six shakes his head. "Nothing mother about this double-dippin' drop out shit," he says under his breath, disappointed about going against the other fisherman for more money.

The crew watches as hoards of fish hit the net. The sun touches the horizon and layers the sky with gold, pink, and red.

"What in the hell is that?" Lando says, pointing towards the shore.

The crew looks. Lights outline the coastline at regular intervals.

"Stay alert!" Torden shouts.

The crew continues working but still watches the beautiful flashing lights on the shore, which add light to the sparkling salmon flooding in powerful waves below the boat. The bay is quiet except for the first stars, the moon, their single boat, and the lights on the coast.

The lights distract Torden, but he attempts to stay focused on running the boat. The salmon are so thick he can feel the net pulling the powerful boat backward. "Wow. We need power to even stay in pla..."

He suddenly notices one light on the coast is flashing a recognizable pattern. He abruptly stops and watches, transfixed.

"All hands off the net! Hold on!" Torden calls as he reverses to spin in the opposite direction, releasing tension on the net and allowing most of the salmon to escape.

"What the fuck?!" Lando questions.

"Reel in the net! Now!!"

"What is it, captain?!" Six asks.

Torden doesn't respond. He stares at the coast. He and the crew hear a low chanting.

"They're singing," Six says.

The women on the coast each have a light at the shoreline, but their nets are not in the water in solidarity for the fishing boats. They sing in a beautiful chanting style as they flash a mirror over their lanterns. The lights on the coast transfix Torden. The beautiful mermaid siren-like sounds call to him.

"What is it?" Six asks again, concerned. He touches Torden's arm.

Torden comes out of it, "She knows my name."

"Torden!" Lando shouts. We've lost most of the fish! What's up, dumb ass? Of all the stupid..."

Torden looks at the coastline. He looks at Lando.

"Get those fish off! Throw them back!"

"What?!!" Lando shouts.

Six and the other crew members follow his instructions, throwing the live salmon back in the bay. Lando stands watching, fuming. "You've gone fuckin' mad!"

"Six, get the immersion suits," Torden commands.

"What?!" Lando questions.

"Now!"

Six opens the hatch and pulls out the full head and body insulated suits meant for emergencies when the boat is in distress.

"Get your suits on!"

Six and the two other crew members immediately put on the bright red immersion suits.

"There's no danger here!" Lando says, his face red, standing in place.

"I'm the captain. Get the goddamn suit on."

Torden pulls his suit on, then accelerates and heads

straight towards the coast. He turns to Six, standing next to him, "Tell the other crew to hold on tight."

Lando reluctantly puts his immersion suit on as he berates Torden for leaving the fish. Torden picks up speed as he gets closer to the coast. Lando stands near the starboard side of the boat, continuing his loud, whiny insults, "You idiotic, wimpy son of a..."

Torden quickly turns the wheel left. Lando flies off the boat and catches hold of the rail. He hangs nearly horizontal off the side for a second. "Help!!"

The crew stays put. Lando shoots off into the water. Torden makes eye contact with Karima holding a lantern on the shore, smiles, then speeds up and turns back towards the other fisherman and the mine.

Lando crawls out of the water on the shore in his immersion suit, angry and swearing. Exhausted from swimming, he stomps out with gusto in front of the women. He stumbles. Karima covers her mouth in a chuckle.

CHAPTER 38
MOSQUITO LARVAE {CULICIDAE}

Sacred prayers and small nuisances sustain hope in a seemingly hopeless fight, as gold and copper are just within reach of the pointed-nail claws of unbridled greed.

Reina calls Amak with a diagram of the bucket-wheel excavator in her hand. There is a hand-drawn red heart around a small part on the console of the operator's cab.

Vovo cruises in the Scout with a mosquito hood over her head. She pulls out survey stakes and throws them into the Scout. Hiking through the bush, she pulls more stakes, throwing them on the ground.

A woman with a black dog in a dusty blue Chevy pretends to break down on a narrow road near the mine site. She shrugs and throws up her hands as a frustrated Boreal Extraction driver is unable to get through behind her.

Amak and helpers sneak into the groundbreaking party location on Iliana Lake and spread scented lotion on the undersides of the party tables.

Frida sits on the shore of Lake Bijou Nez in Sandglass as a group of Alaska Native elders sits in a circle chanting near Bristle Bay. Clouds come into view, and thunder is heard in the distance.

CHAPTER 39

GREAT SLIPPERSNAIL
{CREPIDULA GRANDIS}

Five Alaska Supreme Court Justices face Chalky, Tilly, and Sloane at the front of the courtroom. As Chalky speaks to them, Tilly turns around repeatedly, looking at the door. Chalky calls Tilly up to the bench. She walks up as slowly as she can, stalling.

Suddenly the door opens, and Camas runs in with a manila envelope in hand. Tilly motions excitedly for Camas to join them. A grey-haired man with black-framed glasses, Justice Templeton, nods to the bailiff to allow Tilly to take the document. She hands it to Justice Templeton, who reviews it briefly, then passes it down to Justice Reidy, a black woman in her fifties with a friendly face.

"What is the source of this first right of refusal from Boreal Extraction to Oro Sangriente?" Justice Reidy asks.

"I am uncertain of the provenance, Your Honor," Chalky responds.

"We can't consider this as evidence without knowing the source."

"We found out about the existence of the document from an Oro Sangriente employee," Tilly says.

122

"Where's that employee?" Justice Templeton asks.

"I'm sorry, Your Honor. He's not here."

"Until you can provide that witness, we can't use this. We'll reconvene..."

Tilly interrupts, "But there's no time, they're breaking ground tonight!"

"I'm sorry, young lady," Justice Reidy says gently.

Tilly's head sinks. Camas puts her arm around her.

"We will reconvene upon..."

Suddenly, the back door of the courtroom opens, and Aila Abzug walks in. She wears a tight-fitting red dress and red high heel shoes. She walks with a very hippy swing up the aisle, then confers with Chalky.

"Your honors, we have another document that proves that Oro Sangriente is in a side deal for phase two of the Copper Cobra mine," Chalky announces.

Aila smiles sweetly at the justices.

Torden races with his remaining crew to join the other boats. Six, now a proud partner, pulls a thick red Sharpie out of his pocket and colors his index finger red. He hands it to Torden, who does the same, then throws the marker back to another crewman. They raise their red fingers to fellow fishermen as they reach the tail end of the flotilla.

Dew hobnobs with a group of about 200 investors and Alaskan dignitaries gathered at the dinner and groundbreaking ceremony on Lake Iliana, near the site of the Copper Cobra mine. The guests have a beautiful sunset view, and there are string lights in the trees and lovely chamber music playing. Men in expensive resort attire and women in elegant cocktail dresses hold wine glasses and cocktails. Dew arrives and parks on the edge of the parking lot to leave ahead of the crowd. Dark clouds float in over the river.

CHAPTER 40

PINK SALMON
{ONCHORHYNCHUS GORBUSCHA}

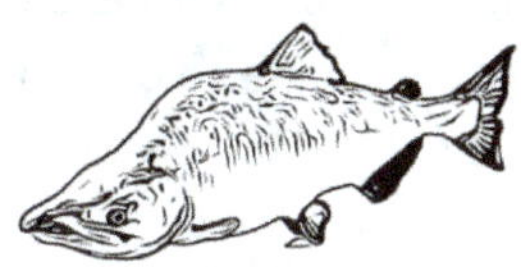

The fishing boats arrive at the mouth of the Kojack River and begin to travel up towards Lake Iliana. Moore answers his phone, standing on Jake's boat, which is among the others at the front of the fleet.

"The guests are arriving. I just sat down, and it says the permit presentation and groundbreaking is at 11:00 pm after dessert," Amak tells Moore in a hushed voice.

"We're at the mouth and heading up."

"There's a lot of shallow water in that river. I don't know if you'll be able to get through."

"I'll let captain Jake know. Peace."

Moore looks at his phone and sees a text from Tilly. *Got the injunction! Check your email! Please confirm.*

Moore texts back. *Roger. Got it! Over.*

"They got the injunction!" Moore says, handing his phone to Spit. "Captain's in the galley. Go print this in the wheelhouse. Fast!"

Spit pulls himself up the railing as he races up the stairs three steps at a time.

The press rolls in. Helicopters from Anchorage news fly overhead as a social media buzz of hundreds of thousands of red pointer fingers explodes online. A female reporter travels on a fishing boat. The boats are close to one another as they travel up the mouth of the river.

"Captain, permission to speak," Moore calls out.

"I'm trying to maneuver here, Moore. Not now!"

"Two critical things."

"Go!"

"Amak says the waters are too low to get through."

"Damn it all."

"I'm sorry, captain."

"What else?"

"Tilly got an injunction from the Supreme Court, but we need to get it to Amak before they turn over the permit. They're doing the ceremony at 11 pm."

"That's an hour and a half. We're 50 miles away, and our fastest boats could get there at full speed in a little over an hour if we can get through."

From a bird's-eye view, deep in the Alaskan bush, a speck of a camera rests on a tripod set up at the base of the enormous Bagger 300 waiting for party guests to witness the groundbreaking.

Spit stands behind Moore and gives him a shove.

"Why are you still standing here?" Jakes says, annoyed.

"What about Torden's boat," Moore blurts out. "He could get through."

The female news reporter's hair blows in the gusty wind. "Around 1,500 fishing boats are heading up the Kojack river towards the Copper Cobra mine. They've abandoned their fishing season to stop Boreal Extraction. This boat's captain is on the radio. There's talk of shallow water ahead."

"That pompous, self-aggrandizing, arrogant twerp. He couldn't do a helpful thing if his life depended on it."

Jake and the crew hear a loud scrape as a boat up ahead suddenly hits bottom and is jarred to a stop. A handful of other boats swerve to miss it and shallow water abruptly stops the boats further up the river. The reporter's boat rear-ends a vessel just a few yards in front of Jake's.

Jake is silent and lowers his head for a moment. He looks Moore and Spit in the eye and picks up his radio.

"Black Jake's Sail to Torden's Catch. Over," he says firmly.

The boys are anxious. Tana and Rod stand below the wheelhouse listening.

"Torden here. Over."

"The river's too low. We've got an injunction to deliver to Iliana to stop the mine groundbreaking. Can you get through? Over."

"I can get through."

"Meet me at the east side of the river at Levelix dock."

"Roger."

The mine celebration gets more festive as wine flows, and catering staff, flown in from Anchorage, serve an elaborate dinner. Dick and Dew sit at a table near the podium. Guests scratch and swat mosquitoes away.

"We've got mosquito traps and citronella, what's with the goddamn mosquitos!" Dick asks Dew, swatting. There are two empty seats with unused plates and settings next to Dick. "And where the hell is Bart?!"

Dew is oblivious, smiling, drinking his cocktail, talking to an elegant woman seated next to him.

"Of course. You don't give a shit. You're already taking your bag of money to the bank." Then adds under his breath, "Asshole."

The sky darkens as thunder booms in the distance.

CHAPTER 41
SOCKEYE SALMON
{ONCORHYNCHUS NERKA}

Torden's boat races at full speed and maneuvers through the other fishing boats. The boats have received a radio call about Torden's mission, and part to make a clear path, red pointer fingers raised. Torden pulls up fast to Jake's boat. Spit quickly leans over the edge and hands Torden a paper in a plastic ziplock bag.

"This needs to get to Amak before they hand over the permit!" Moore shouts.

"Got it!" Torden jumps back to the wheel. He calls to his crew. "Listen up! I'll be cruising at full speed through the Kojack through six-inch waters in some spots. I haven't ever run this river, but I have every intention of getting to Iliana. Anyone who wants out, now's the time!"

Two crewmen shrug and climb out and over to Jake's boat.

Spit looks at Moore. The two of them jump over to Torden's boat. They look at Jake with wide eyes. He stands up straight and gives them a warm smile and a salute. Six shakes their hands warmly.

"Godspeed!" Jake shouts.

"Hold on!" Torden accelerates to full power and races off between the remaining boats to an empty river.

Six Alaska Native women of various ages in traditional dress walk to the front of the groundbreaking gathering.

Dick takes the microphone in hand. "In honor of our deep respect for the Native people of this area,"

A dancer rolls her eyes to another.

"...we have the Lake Iliana dance group here tonight."

The guests applaud politely. The dancers begin a slow traditional dance and chant behind an Alaskan elder with long grey hair and a face lined with stories of the land. She recites along with hand movements.

"Iliana Lake is the largest lake in Alaska and covers 1,000 square miles and is 1,000 feet deep." She makes an arc over her head with her hands and sweeps them down low. "Through the river, its waters drain into Bristle Bay. Iliana is said to be the name of a mythical great blackfish."

The dancers make an ominous sound.

She makes a rowing motion, "It inhabits this lake and bites holes in the bidarkas of the bad people."

The dancers make another ominous noise.

"Let's get this dog and pony show on the road so we can get the goddamn permit," Dew complains to Dick.

"We're pacifying the press. Only a few more minutes and we start up the Bagger," Dick says as he texts to the cameraman and crew at the mine. *Get ready to start-up and film in five.*

A young man in the operating seat near the startup button for the Bagger reads the text and gets in position to start up the monolithic earth destroyer.

Torden pushes the boat fast, painstakingly making his way up the river, swerving to miss the lowest spots. The crew grimaces and holds on tight when they hear the bottom brush the river floor now and again.

Torden turns around to the crew. "She's got to fly faster! Hold on!!"

Torden picks up even more speed to retain the ground effect of the hydroplane.

"Looks like only one boat is trying to get through..." a news commentator says.

Jake is near the front of all of the boats with radio in hand. "It's too shallow up here. Torden is delivering an important document. Stand by. Spread the word."

Jake takes off his cap, shoes, and fishing overalls. He wears swim trunks underneath and has a salmon tattoo on his strong upper shoulder. "Tana, call Blackfish Lodge and tell them I'll need a room tonight. A hammock will do if they're full up. Rod, take the boat to Nawgek when you get news from Torden."

"What are you doing, Captain?" Rod asks.

"Something I've wanted to do for 35 years." He jumps into the water and starts swimming.

"It's over a mile upstream! Jake!!" Rod shouts.

CHAPTER 42
BALD EAGLE {HALIAAETUS LEUCOCEPHALUS}

Dew walks up to the podium as the dancers finish. Rain begins to come down on the guests. They applaud and lift programs over their head, sipping wine and cocktails with their other hand.

"This is a landmark moment. The wealth of these lands will find their way to their true destiny."

The crowd nods and smiles. A motor rumbles in the distance over sounds of thunder.

"Please welcome EPA Director, Prewitt Mountain, Deputy Director, Reina McCaring, and Army Corps of Engineers Environmental Director, Beatrice Laurels."

There is a very faint chanting in the background. Alaska Natives surround the elegant party with sacred prayers in the forest.

"Thank you, Dew. It's a pleasure to be in this beautiful setting," Bea says. She raises a piece of paper ceremoniously. "I have here..."

Torden's powerful motor roars over Bea's words. Dew, Prewitt, Reina, and Bea turn around, and the crowd gasps as the boat travels at full speed towards the guests at the edge of the shore. Dick and the crowd let out screams as they leap up and run from their seats while Amak races the opposite direction towards the boat. The boat bears down, then turns and slides up onto the edge of the shore just in front of Amak.

Moore leaps out into the shallow water and hands Amak the paper. Amak races up the beach and gives it to Bea.

"What in the hell is going on?!" Dick shouts from the lawn.

Bea reads the injunction. "The Supreme Court of Alaska enjoins Boreal Extraction to immediately halt construction and all activities related to Copper Cobra mine."

Reina hugs Amak. Torden, Six, Moore and Spit hug and high-five each other. Amak and Reina wave to Torden and his crew.

Dew is furious and throws his fists down to his sides in anger. Guests stare as he marches across the barren party lawn, kicking chairs and pushing empty tables over. He gets to his SUV covered with black feathers. Smiling faces peer through the shrubs. Furiously, he wipes off his windshield with his dress-shirted forearm and speeds off in a black-feathered car.

A raven flies overhead.

The Alaska Natives chant as they walk back through the forest. They get into trucks and canoes to return home. Animals make beautiful triumphant calls through the night.

Jake swims among thousands and thousands of sockeye salmon along the beautiful river. He laughs as he makes his way upstream.

CHAPTER 43
BELUGA WHALE
{DEPHINAPTERUS LEUCAS}

A modest commercial fishing boat with the name *à la réflexion* painted on the stern sits on Bristle Bay as the sun sets. Bart and Eve, in orange fishing overalls and knit beanies, sit enjoying a romantic picnic with smoked salmon, cheeses, bread, and wine. They lean into each other and have a slow kiss.

Amak paddles a canoe in Lake Iliana with his son behind him. A duffel bag rests at the front of the boat. He hands the oars to his son, unzips the bag, takes a photo, then zips it back up. He takes out his phone and texts.

Amak points to the center of the lake. His son paddles as Amak enjoys the warm sun on his face. Amak picks up the duffel bag and drops it over the side with a plunk.

"What was that?!"

"Just an offering to the blackfish, son."

Reina flyfishes in waders in a beautiful Alaskan stream. Later that afternoon, she sits on the runway in a small puddle jumper airplane on her journey back home. She pulls out her phone and reads Amak's text.

I borrowed the heart.

She smiles.

A beautiful, long, festive table on the lawn of Vovo's riverfront lodge holds flowers, salmon, and other delicacies. Moore, Isla, and Spit dance on the lawn to blues music played by a local acoustic trio. Jake, Rod, and Tana laugh and *talk fish* with Sloane, Heinz, and Amak. Vovo holds Frida's hand as she explains the plants in her garden. Amak's wife keeps an eye on their children playing at the shore. Camas and Josh sneak a kiss, standing on the grass overlooking the river. Torden, Karima, and Six enjoy watching the dancers with a beer in their hands.

A tone as warm and ageless as Vovo sounds as she rings a gong and motions for the group to sit.

Graeme Selkirk, Liam's father, ruggedly handsome with short grey-blonde hair, drives up in Vovo's Scout. He joins the group, shakes his brother Jake's hand, then Black's. He leans down to kiss Vovo on the cheek.

"How was the fishing?" Black asks.

"Just as I remember, Dad," Graeme smiles as he sits down.

The band plays a gentle melody as Tilly and Liam walk out of the lodge down the porch stairs in beautiful white and crème-colored attire with colorful leis. They each kiss Graeme on his cheek and sit at the end of the table opposite of Vovo. Graeme raises his wine glass.

"To the happy couple," Graeme says. "Tilly and Liam, may you swim happily side by side for the rest of your lives."

"And get spawning!" Vovo shouts.

The group laughs and drinks from their glasses in a jubilant celebration.

"Cheers!"

"Prost!"

"Imiqta!"

"Salud!"

The round face of a beluga pops up out of the water. Vovo sees it first and turns to Moore and motions with her head and eyes back to the water. Moore's eyes light up. He pokes Spit and nods with his head towards the beautiful white whale who looks at them playfully. The whale dives under the water then, emerges with a salmon in his mouth, a seeming smile on his face, then dives back under and swims away.

"Is it?" Moore and Spit look to Vovo with questioning eyes.

"Sometimes money *can* buy you happiness," Vovo purrs.

Vovo, Spit, and Moore bob their heads to the blues beat.

THE END

PEDRO'S PRIMER

Tilly asked me to share a few woofs with you.

I'm not sure if you know, but my great, great, great, great, grandfather was a fisherdog in Portugal. My ancestors were working dogs who retrieved nets and untangled lines and stood guard on boats. A monk even wrote down a story of one of my ancestors rescuing a sailor way back in 1927. That is all to say, I have the sea in my DNA.

Just like salmon, I love to swim in clean water. If people let poison flow into the water, all living things will die — fish, dogs, and humans.

I heard my mistress Tilly say once that "without blue, there can be no green."

Do you know what that means?

It means that air should be blue. It means that oceans, lakes, and rivers should be blue.

And then... we can have flowers.

Download a FREE eBook copy of Book 1,
One More Year:
www.AvisKalfsbeek.com/Book1free

Become a Patron to get EARLY chapters and books by the
author, Avis Kalfsbeek:
www.patreon.com/pedrothewaterdog

Prereleased chapters

Behind the scenes

Pedro planet love

Other writings

patreon.com/pedrothewaterdog

Song of Speaks-Fluently

To have to carry your own corn far —
who likes it?
To follow the black bear through the thicket —
who likes it?
To hunt without profit, to return without anything —
who likes it?
You have to carry your own corn far.
You have to follow the black bear.
You have to hunt without profit.
If not, what will you tell the little ones?
What will you speak of?
For it is bad not to use the talk which God has sent us.

I am Speaks-Fluently. Of all the groups of symbols,
I am a symbol by myself.

Poet of the Osage Nation